VIJAY THARIANI

Cover Design by Poonam Thariani

INDIA · SINGAPORE · MALAYSIA

Notion Press Media Pvt Ltd

No. 50, Chettiyar Agaram Main Road,
Vanagaram, Chennai, Tamil Nadu – 600 095

First Published by Notion Press 2021
Copyright © Vijay Thariani 2021
All Rights Reserved.

ISBN 978-1-63873-611-0

I dedicate this book to my late parents

Shri Vithaldas P. Thariani

Smt. Sita V. Thariani

ACKNOWLEDGEMENT

I shall always remain indebted to:

Jaya

Rachana & Ojas Sampat

Poonam & Rachit Thariani

Hansaben & Udaybhai Sampat

*For encouraging me to not give up on my dream
of writing a book. Without their wholehearted support,
it would not have been possible for me to put in the effort
required to complete it.*

Special thanks to my grandchildren:

Parth

Parami

Param

For changing my life and bringing back my childhood.

Heartfelt thanks to my:

Elder brother, Dr Kishan V. Thariani

Sister-In-Law, Shantabhabhi

*For their support in laying a strong foundation
for my future.*

Special thanks to:

Jamnaben and Late Shri Bhagwandas Kesaria

Rekhaben & Naresh Bhatia

*For always being supportive of my interest
in writing this book.*

I am thankful to my:

Sisters, brothers-in-law, sisters-in-law

Friends

Colleagues

Business Associates

**And above all, the countless well-wishers
I have had the good fortune of meeting.**

My special thanks to Dikshita, Renuka, Kavya, Urmi,
Juhi, Rhea, Saheefa, Nishanth and the entire team
of Notion Press for helping me in the process of
publishing the book.

PREFACE

It gives me immense pleasure to put my first book in your hand.

The inspiration for this novel comes from the ten plus years I trained myself to control my emotions while writing. This was necessary to give fair justice to the protagonist – hero of my novel.

The story revolves around the life experiences of my hero. Yet, I would not claim it to be his autobiography, even though it is written in an autobiographical style as he selects only those experiences or incidences through which a message is conveyed. It is for the reader to take a cue from his decisions and actions if placed in similar situations or circumstances.

In this format, there cannot only be a symbolic relationship between the author, the protagonist and the reader. It has to result in a deep bonding between the three of them.

What should the protagonist's name be? I debated several names. It took up a lot of my time. A thought then popped up in my mind – Why can't I lend him my name? And the names of my near and dear ones for the characters that surround him?

So my hero – the main character of the novel is Vijay.

Vijay is simple, kind at heart, principled, sincere, emotional, and conscious of not hurting anyone by written or spoken words or acts. He gets easily disturbed if someone intentionally hurts his feelings and self-respect. Yet he resists being vocal when accusing anyone, preferring silence so others can draw their own interpretation of his thoughts.

At the same time, if he finds that someone has put him in a situation he does not want to be in, he does not carry the burden of malice towards that person. Without any grudge, he helps them when asked.

I am also keen not to reveal the profound secrets of Vijay, who desists from revealing ALL good and bad, sweet and sour happenings in his life. Instead, he prefers to be selective. Vijay maintains personal integrity, to tell the truth gracefully. I have flagged him off on his journey precisely for this reason.

As an author, I want to leave suggested messages in the novel for interpretation, as readers have a more spectacular and remarkable intelligence than the author.

Perceptions of reality never change or lose their value ever, so are the messages sent out by Vijay.

Therefore, my attempt is not to make this novel Vijay's soliloquy but to make him talk to the readers, live.

Vijay candidly says, "I am not a public figure, why would anyone be interested to know, when and where I was born?" Let me not assess my protagonist myself, as I may be tempted to be partial.

In the end, a novel is judged by an individual reader's thinking and emotions – emotions are hard and impossible to quantify.

Let the readers conclude if this novel falls into the fiction or non-fiction category. After all, I do not claim my novel is a reflection of my experiments with truth, but for Vijay it is not far from that.

Criticism and acclamations are welcome.

Vijay Thariani

CHAPTER ONE

After a spectacular viewing of Mount McKinley, Alaska, North America's highest peak at twenty thousand three hundred feet, we landed on a glacier at a height of about seven thousand feet.

Wow! Amazing! Instant reactions from the nine of us. Our five and four-seater planes landed simultaneously.

It was indeed a divine experience. The gentle rays of the sun were pleasant and soothing. While flying between the mountain ranges, I thought of the Himalayan range. Even though I have never experienced flying there, I remembered childhood stories of the Land of God as seen in movies and pictures.

We were given 20 minutes to enjoy the spectacular Alaskan majesty.

After a brief photo session, my son-in-law Ojas, his brother Anuj and their father Udaybhai were taking picturesque shots from various angles. My daughter Rachana, grandchildren Parth and Parami, my wife Jaya and Udaybhai's wife Hansaben were throwing snowballs at each other. We missed my son, Rachit, and daughter-in-law Poonam. My grandson, Param had not been born as yet.

And what was I doing? My ecstatic reactions evaporated. The thrill of landing on a glacier was short-lived.

I think…I was searching for the child within me…I was supposed to have the heart of a poet to witness such spectacular sights. But I could not find it. Had it slipped into a coma? Had my feelings slipped into deep unconsciousness?

Had I witnessed such a beautiful charming sight a few years ago, I would have danced and cried tears of joy. I probably would have written or recited a few poetic lines praising nature.

I have always believed that the first two or three lines are considered God's gift. But that was not to be. It was not happening. Maybe God too was not in a mood to part ways with that precious gift. I made a frantic attempt to awaken the child within me. I knew the child was there but not responding. I kept trying. Alas! I failed and miserably at that. After about five minutes of my failed search, I heard Rachana call me. "Pappa, what are you doing there? Come, join us and enjoy." I suddenly realized that I had spent much of the 20 minutes allotted to us, remaining aloof, trying too hard to find what was evasive.

Before turning around, I wiped my misty eyes and joined them. Somehow I managed not to allow my inner agony to be reflected on my generally expressive face. I made sure that no one would ask me what had happened. I thought to myself that happiness and sadness are not measurable as parameters, they are vulnerable to unnatural sensitivity.

CHAPTER TWO

We returned to base after spending 25 minutes more than the allotted time. I was not myself. I was stunned and surprised by my failure to locate my poetic heart and the child within me. I kept thinking of my rare failure on this front on the way back home. I was concerned that I was becoming numb, that I had lost my heart and my emotions. Would any joyous or sad event not move me anymore?

While I was lost in thought, I was reminded of a childhood incident when I saw a pigeon sitting on my window sill. I imagined pigeons being harassed by humans. And within five minutes, I wrote a prize-winning poem on cruelty towards pigeons.

When John F. Kennedy was assassinated, I wrote and spoke on his achievements as President of the USA; writings and speeches that won acclamations in school competitions.

In school, college, and at work, I had written poetry, essays and other literary works, either for self-enjoyment or for competitions.

Had all these creative activities come to an end? My once unbounded creativity was lost or hiding somewhere deep within.

I was in a state of mild depression and disappointment for a few days. Suddenly, a thought occurred to me. Before the wings of my imagination were further clipped, what if I wrote a memoir? To avoid reaching an unknown impasse?

The very thought cheered me up.

CHAPTER THREE

I immediately resolved that I would write it. This decision brought me great relief.

But why should I call it an autobiography as it will be selective? I asked myself, "Who would be interested in my memoir and why should they be interested in my life?" I was not a public figure or super achiever in any specialised field. Why should someone care about when and where I was born, how many siblings I had, where I spent my childhood? Other than for my self-satisfaction, what was my purpose in penning my memoir?

I got my answer from within.

After all, I was involved in social activities from the time I was a teenager. I had been a first-year college dropout, a bank clerk, then a college graduate, a bank executive and then a jeweller.

What if I inked those experiences which by themselves might send relevant messages to the readers? Under the given circumstances, I might have taken certain decisions with an outcome that I may or may not have desired. How did they affect my life? How did I decide? What did I learn from them? If I wrote about such incidents and faced similar circumstances, perhaps my writing could provide some guidance and help somebody in their personal and/or professional life.

I talked with Jaya, Udaybhai, Ojas, Rachit, Rachana, Poonam, and Hansaben, about my decision to write a memoir. Whenever I shared my life experiences with them, they suggested I write them. When I shared some of my experiences with my friends, even they would encourage me to write a memoir. I was sharing some of the pleasant and painful life experiences with family and few friends and asking them whether it would be worth writing a book. They were on the same page and encouraged me to go ahead.

Yet, I was thinking and taking time to decide. I wanted to write the truth and as we all know; the truth is sometimes hurtful. I would need to take utmost care to ensure that my memoir did not become a soliloquy. It should also not hurt anyone. But would I be able to avoid not hurting anybody? Probably yes, if I chose my words carefully. Words matter. They have the power to create or destroy, don't they?

After about a year or so of intense self-deliberation, I decided to write a memoir for the benefit of myself, for those whom I know and also for those who may wish to know a little bit about my life.

The first dilemma I faced – where do I begin?

A memoir is not a personal diary. It is not meant only on the instances an individual encounters in his or her private, professional and social life. I had to be selective in choosing incidents, allotting them the appropriate space, in line with my intention to send out relevant messages. I resolved to be extremely sensitive in not overstating or exaggerating obvious elements in my journey.

CHAPTER FOUR

As mentioned earlier, I decided to write only about those experiences which would send out learning on success or failure in personal, professional and social life. And also because I was not a public figure, I wanted to share my journey with circumstances leading to the start of my professional career.

I must make a mention here, all that I write may not be in chronological order as sometimes, somewhere in between I might have to delve into the past. I seek pardon for this, but I will remain committed to incorporating only those incidents which send out a message or two.

So, here I go…Resolving to keep my aspirations modest.

My S.S.C.E. (Std. XI in those days) results were just out. I secured a second class. And yet, I was as excited as if I had secured a distinction. I had been scared of failing, particularly in mathematics which was my least favourite subject. I had no clue about geometrical theorems.

I never understood them or more truthfully, never tried to understand how to prove a statement to be true or false. Geometry consists of a set of theorems, each derived from definitions, axioms and it represents truths without formal proof, called postulate – statements assumed to be true without proof. Like they say, truth does not need any witness or oath!

In a moment of excitement, my father asked the question every college-ready child dreads. "What do you want to do next?" Before I could even think (as if I was going to), my elder brother suggested I take up science and aim to be a doctor – just like him.

Caught up in the moment, I agreed. I did not realize that I had no liking for maths, biology, chemistry and physics. I had forgotten that I cleared my math exam only by memorising theorems like memorising poems, instead of logically proving them. I did not think for a second that in the examination hall, while answering theorem questions, I had first written the entire text and drawn the figures last, as opposed to first drawing the figures and then proving the statement. Even as I wrote, the supervisor was amazed and leant over me to make sure I was not cheating.

My father was the only earning member of our family and had to work hard. So was the case all around us. Elders hardly had any time to think about or judge their child's potential. My brother sincerely felt that I should go on to become a doctor like him. I enrolled for a degree in science.

However, with the core science subjects not being my natural choice, my focus shifted to extra-curricular activities – sports and cultural events. I became the sports secretary with a special interest in playing cricket. Soon thereafter, I was selected as captain of the college cricket team. We played several competitive tournaments. I was instrumental in organising some unique events to celebrate "College Week". My suggestion to play a cricket match between the students and the professors and employees of the college was accepted. It was considered to be a unique event those days.

While I was excelling in extracurricular activities, I neglected my studies. I was never punctual in attending lectures or practicals. I was irregular in attending classes.

The inevitable happened.

CHAPTER FIVE

As our qualifying exams approached, my college principal called for me.

"Look, Vijay, it is a practice in this college to allow secretaries of various activities to appear for the qualifying exams irrespective of their mandatory attendance and periodic test performance. Start working hard for the exams, will you?"

I thanked him and asked if I could meet him again the next day. He agreed and invited me to walk in any time.

I went home thinking, probably for the first time in my life, about what would happen if I appeared for the qualifying exams and failed. Failing the exams was the most likely, actually no, a certain outcome. I could probably catch up with the theoretical part, but what about my practicals? Joining private classes was not an option because of my financial situation.

What should I do? Should I accept it as a challenge? Even if I accept it, the chances of success were close to zero. I had not built any base upon which my academic future could stand.

Should I talk to my brother? My father? To my two elder sisters or my younger sister?

Now I realized that I had impulsively opted for science without evaluating my ability or interest. I asked myself whether it was important for elders in the family to know a child's real interest and potential.

If I confided in my father and brother, they would be disappointed. The thought of their disappointment scared me more than the surety of their anger.

There were still a few hours left for my father to come back from work. My brother was in the hostel, busy with the gruelling demands of his medical course. We did not have a telephone at home. I felt lonely. My mother was always busy with household work. We hardly had any leisurely communication within the family. I was not yet 18. I did not have a single friend whom I could turn to. I wept profusely.

After finishing her *pooja* (prayers), my mother asked me, "What happened Vijay? Why are you crying? Are you okay? Is anything happening to you? Any problems in college?"

I raised my head but could not look into her eyes. Finally, in a low voice, I shared my conversation with the Principal. She listened and asked me to talk to my father when he came home. In a caring tone, she asked me to stop crying and to eat something.

My father came home and finished his dinner. Just as he was about to start reading a book, his daily routine after dinner, I told him in a subdued tone about my conversation with the college Principal. He listened intently, and I could see he was upset. After I was done, he asked, "So, what do you want to do?"

I responded, "*Bha*, (which is how we addressed him) I don't think I will be able to clear the exams. I am thinking of telling the Principal that I will not be able to sit for the exams." I also shared with *Bha* that I spent most of my time in college with other activities. My attendance in practicals was not even ten per cent, and I was irregular in attending lectures.

I could see him struggling to resist an outburst. His eyes conveyed his feelings. Those days, we read and understood the language of the eyes. He was upset, angry, disappointed. I waited. Every passing second appeared to me like a minute and every minute an hour.

I cursed myself for my childish approach to my education. It was a negligent and unpardonable mistake. I was grossly irresponsible.

A thousand thoughts, all of them scary and spine chilling went through my mind. It was a nerve-wracking wait.

After about five minutes, he said in a low but angered tone, "Okay, inform your Principal that you will not be appearing in the exams. We will talk again tomorrow."

I wanted to feel relieved, but my conscience would not allow me to feel that way. It was a blunder. Why did

I not, even once, during the whole year, think of this eventuality? It is not encouraging to start a career with a monumental failure. I tried to find the words to console myself or probably tried to find excuses. It was futile.

The next day I went to the Principal and told him that after speaking with my father, I had decided not to appear in the exams as I was convinced that I would not be able to clear them even with minimum marks.

The Principal looked at me in disbelief. He stared at me for a minute and said "Are you sure you don't want to even attempt it?"

"Sir, maybe I will be able to catch up with the theory, but what about practicals? No sir, I do not want to lie to you that I will try my best. Even if somehow I manage to clear the exams this time, Sir, I don't think I can become a doctor, ever. Which was the intention with which I opted for science."

He tried to persuade me. He even lauded my performance in extracurricular activities. He shared that he and his colleagues had high regard for me for managing all events well below the allocated budget and refunding the balance to the college, something that had never happened in the history of the college. They thought of me as their rising, bright star.

With moist eyes, I thanked him for his compliments. "Sir, I am sorry to disappoint you. With all sincerity and honesty, I am telling you that I will not be able to clear the exams. Let me see what destiny has in store for me."

He appreciated my honesty. "You are the only person to date to have said this in my tenure as a college principal. Okay, best of luck. But please do attend my last address to the faculty and the students before the end of the academic year." I agreed.

In his address, he called me to the dais. Holding my hand, he said, "You all know him. Vijay is our sports secretary and cricket captain. He has excelled on and off the field. I am sad to announce that Vijay has willingly opted out of appearing for the qualifying exams. He says he is certain of his failure. I feel sorry for his decision. Such a decision by a student is rare – something I have not witnessed. However, friends, let us all stand up and appreciate him for his honesty and courage to take such a decision."

Loud applause broke out and I could not control my tears.

Despite the guilt of wasting an entire year, I felt a sense of pride and satisfaction. My honesty was hailed and acknowledged.

Did I deserve this? I was not sure.

I knew I had learnt an important lesson – to not avoid the truth, however painful.

CHAPTER SIX

In the evening, I went home and briefed my father. He was upset but did not utter a word. He said we will talk in the morning.

I tried to sleep but was unable to. I was tossing and turning, moving around restlessly in bed. All I could think of was "what next".

At about 2 a.m. I got up to drink water. The eight of us, including my grandmother, lived in a small one-bedroom flat.

I heard my father and mother talking about our family's financial challenges and wondering how they would get by. I distinctly remember my mother saying, "Don't worry, we will sell my gold bangles."

I was shattered and felt like crying out loud. What had I done? I had wasted an entire year and also the money spent on my college fees. I cursed myself. I realized I should do something for the family. But what could I do at this age, especially when I was not even able to clear my first year in college?

The next morning, I waited for my father to talk to me. He did not utter a single word. I could not muster the courage to ask him whether and what he wanted to talk to me about. Perhaps his priority was to arrange for the funds that I overheard him talking to my mother about last night.

Fifteen days passed amidst anxiety and restlessness. Even though my father did not speak a single word about me, I could see several questions in his eyes.

Another fifteen days passed in the same way. One evening, he came back from the bank where he worked, and even before changing, he asked me: "So, what do you want to do now?"

I did not have a good answer and responded, "As you say."

He said that his bank was hiring children of staff members. No written test was required, only an interview. The minimum required qualification was S.S.C.E., which I had.

"Do you want to work?"

"As you say." I again said.

Immediately he said that it would be of help to the family.

I promptly responded that I was ready.

That instant decision to be employed was so satisfying, that even today, I am unable to describe it in words. I had grown up and learnt that maturity was not when we start talking about the big things, but instead it was when we start understanding the small things.

CHAPTER SEVEN

The very next day, I filled out my first job application, of course, dictated by my father. I signed it. He planned to submit it after 15 days when I would become a 'major' or 18 years old. I realized I had now committed myself to the professional path. I could no longer even think about switching from Science to Arts or Commerce – at least for now.

A fortnight later, I was called for a personal interview. Having never attended a job interview, I was tense, but not nervous. I was told the interview would be about testing my general knowledge.

Fortunately, since the time I was in the seventh grade, I had developed the habit of reading and writing. I read fiction as well as weekly and monthly magazines, which typically contained a general knowledge section. But they were all in Gujarati, the medium of instruction in my school. However, I conversed in English with my teammates in the cricket team. They were all at least four to five years older than me.

I must make a special mention here of my seventh grade English teacher, Mr Kharas, a kind and elderly Parsi gentleman. In those days, if you were a student of a vernacular language school, you did not start learning

English until seventh grade. And so, I started learning my A, B, C's at the age of 13.

I was not able to attend school on my second day. When I went on the third day, Kharas Sir asked me where I was the previous day. I spoke my first sentence in English, "Sir, I am absent."

The entire class burst into laughter. But not Kharas Sir. He said, "Son, say I was absent. 'Was' is past tense and 'am' is present tense, the now. So, what would you say?"

"Sir, I was absent."

Kharas Sir acknowledged my correction. From there on, for reasons not known to me, he started taking a keen interest in my progress. He would ask me to read paragraphs from different pages of textbooks, to speak on different topics based on what I had understood from my reading. He went even further and asked me to see him in the staff room during recess if I needed additional help.

Gradually, I became more confident about speaking and writing in English. I was now able to read a few English periodicals, literature, general knowledge books and books on other subjects.

I was always fond of reading interviews of sportspersons and politicians and was fascinated by the tricky questions they were asked. Little did I realize how this would help me during my first ever job interview.

Thank you, Kharas Sir, from the bottom of my heart. Please bless me forever from wherever you are. You were a good teacher, not only in how you explained, but how you inspired.

The evening before my interview, my father asked me if I had been reading newspapers and general knowledge books.

I assured him I did.

He asked if I was nervous. I answered in the negative.

He asked if I was confident. I said yes.

He advised, "Be confident, but not overconfident. Be polite."

He gave me a few helpful tips like any concerned father would. Everything from when my name was called to the opening of the door of the interview room, greeting the panel, not to sit until asked to do so, how to thank and wish the panel when the interview was complete and even how to close the door while stepping out.

I listened to the instructions carefully and fully intended to follow them to the T.

He then said that my selection was assured unless I proved to be dumb or showed a complete lack of manners or if I was rude or did not know the answers to the questions.

His final instruction to me was, "Don't bluff if you do not know the answer. Instead say, I am sorry sir, I do not know the answer. Vijay, this is a panel interview comprising three members. Each member will ask you questions related to different fields. When one person is asking you questions, the other two will be observing you closely. They will be assessing your personality. How you answer and how much time you take to answer each question. Are you bluffing? Are you confident? If you don't know the answer, don't bluff. Don't provide additional details if not asked. Keeping these factors in mind, each panellist will mark you individually. The chairman of the interview panel is the Assistant General Manager of the bank, Mr Vinay Daftari. The other two members are Mr Persi Daruwalla and Mr Sachin Vicharekar. I have spoken to Mr Daftari. He told me, 'Mr Thariani, why are we interviewing children of the staff? Unless someone is rubbish, we will appoint all of them'."

My father had a stellar reputation in the bank. I knew I had to do well to preserve it.

My father continued. "Now listen carefully, Vijay. Mr Daftari is a soft-spoken person. You have to be attentive. He does not like to repeat himself. If you say 'I beg your pardon' more than twice, he will not appreciate it. He is also known to ask at least one question that tests a candidate's presence of mind. There is no set pattern. The topic could be history, geography, general knowledge or it could be a personal question. So be alert and attentive."

This made me nervous. For the first time, I felt conscious about being a student of Gujarati medium, except for the one year in college that I wasted. Would I be able to do well in an interview conducted in English? I prayed.

Finally, the day arrived. My father left early. I sensed some anxiety on his face. Before leaving, he instructed me on what to wear and asked me to get to the bank at least an hour before the scheduled time – 5 p.m.

As instructed, I reached the office at 4 p.m. trying hard to preserve the creases of my well-ironed clothes in the crowded local train.

The minimum age to qualify for the job was 18. It was just 10 days since my 18th birthday.

I prepared myself to grab this opportunity. It was knocking at my door. I was determined not to lose it.

CHAPTER EIGHT

At around 4:30 p.m. an official with a French beard came through the doors and greeted the interviewees – 12 in all. He shook hands with each of us, perhaps because we were children of staff members.

I thought he shook my hand for a little longer than the others. Did I imagine that or was it because I was the son of a senior officer? Maybe, I thought.

He had a list of the names of candidates which he verified with the interview letters.

I wasn't expecting to be the first one to be called. "Mr Thariani, you are the first candidate to be interviewed today. Are you prepared?" I answered in the affirmative.

At exactly 5 p.m. he called my name and signalled that I could go into the interview room.

For a split second, I was nervous but immediately gathered myself.

I knocked on the door and opened it slightly.

"May I come in, sir?"

"Come in."

Thanking everyone, I went in and stood before the candidate chair.

"Please sit down."

Again thanking everyone, I took a seat.

I looked at the panel members. I had never even seen a photograph of Mr Daftari. He was flanked by two other executives. Because he was in the centre, I presumed he would lead the interview.

The three gentlemen glanced at each other.

Mr Daftari asked the first question.

"What is your name?"

I was briefly perplexed by the question. He had my application in front of him. Without wasting time, I said, "Vijay Vithaldas Thariani."

"Are you related to Mr V.P. Thariani?"

Surprised at the simplicity of the question, I instantly replied, "Yes sir, he is my father."

"WHAT!" said Mr Daftari, sounding angry and stern at the same time.

I knew I had bungled the response. But what could I have gotten wrong with such a basic question? Without wasting more time, I corrected myself "Sorry sir, I am his son."

I truly believe God put these words in my mouth. Mr Daftari smiled and said "No more questions from me."

He gestured to the other two panellists that it was their turn. I sensed they were surprised, and dare I say, impressed.

Sitting to the right of Mr Daftari was Mr Vicharekar, who I remembered my father informing me, was transferred from Africa just the previous week. While the two of them had not interacted yet, they knew each other by name and position.

His first question surprised me, "Who is the President of North Vietnam?" I did not know the answer and replied as such. And stupidly, ignoring my father's advice to not provide details if not asked, I added that I was not interested in politics.

He immediately responded that his question was about general knowledge and not about politics.

I got scared and nervous.

Unexpectedly, Mr Daftari came to my rescue. "Mr Vicharekar, he has just become a major. He is quite young to be interested in all fields."

I sighed with relief.

Not wanting to go against his senior, Mr Vicharekar made light of things saying that he was just pulling my leg. Thereafter, he asked simple general knowledge questions, which I was able to answer.

Now, it was the turn of the third executive on the panel, Mr Daruwalla. All smiles, he asked me which school I had studied in. I said I studied in a municipal school till sixth grade, and from seventh to tenth grade at Bharda New High School. I added that I had passed my S.S.C.E from a Gujarati medium school near my house.

As it turned out, he was an ex-Bhardaite, so was happy to hear the name of his alma mater. He enquired about the Principal and a few teachers. Then the conversation turned to cricket, a topic of intent mutual interest for both of us.

He asked many questions about cricket. One of them was to name five cricketers and their key achievements of the West Indian team, then touring India. I answered the questions on cricket confidently and correctly.

After this, Mr Daftari said, "You may go now."

"Thank you, sir, Goodnight sir", I responded as tutored. As I was leaving, I thanked him from the bottom of my heart for coming to my rescue when I had no clue about the answer to the question about the North Vietnamese president. I wondered why he did so. Was it because I promptly corrected my answer to his question? Maybe.

This made me realize, that in the bank I was to be known as my father's son and not the other way around. It also taught me about the importance of respecting elders.

Once again I thanked God for putting these words in my mouth, "Sorry sir, I am his son."

When I got home, my father was waiting for me. I gave him all the details. He said, "Good. Should not be any problem."

When he came back from the office the next day, he informed me that I had topped the batch of interviewees. Mr Daftari was happy with me for instantly correcting my answer.

"Congratulations," he patted me on my back.

I was excited and I had learnt a lesson in my life. Sometimes, questions that appear simple, do not have straightforward answers. In fact, with some discerning, one realizes that the true meaning behind these questions and the complexity of the correct answer.

My siblings were also happy for me. My brother, whom I affectionately called *Adha*, while happy, was disappointed because he sincerely wanted me to become a doctor. Sorry *Adha*, for not choosing the path you thought of for me.

Now it was up to me to unlock my abilities, to not only improve my attitude but also decide my career altitude.

CHAPTER NINE

I joined the bank. Perhaps, I was the youngest in the entire banking industry at that time – 18 years and 20 days at a monthly salary of Rs. 236/-. It was decided by my father that my railway pass + Rs. 25/- as monthly pocket money would be deducted from my salary and the balance would go to the family kitty. This gave me great satisfaction. I had one overarching aim in life at that time – to be good, not for the sake of being good, but also being good for something worthy.

I felt that all of a sudden, I had grown up, no longer the boy who played cricket, but a man with a sense of responsibility. I had to now behave appropriately and responsibly in the bank and even outside of it, to ensure that my father's and my family's name was not tarnished. I also knew that, among all my friends, I was the only one who had a job and was earning a salary. While I considered it to be a matter of pride, I had to take utmost care of not developing an attitude.

After a few days, when I went to open a staff salary account where my monthly salary was to be credited, the clerk behind the counter jocularly commented "Hey, did you also use your influence to get an account number?"

I had no clue what he meant. He said, "Your account number is 1234, a special one allocated to you." We both burst out laughing. At that moment, I resolved that I would apply for a promotion only after my father retired. I followed through on that promise to myself.

That I was contributing to my family was a satisfying feeling. But was I sacrificing my youth and my dreams? Was this the end of the light, playful days that are an important part of any youth's life? And, what of my formal education? I did not have answers to these questions at that moment but had faith that my future would answer them.

My job scenario was almost the same as it would be in any other office, I thought. Being the son of a senior bank executive, I knew I was pampered. Many of my colleagues were soft towards me. I also knew that some of them were grumbling about the preferential treatment I was receiving. Other than that, life was going smoothly by the hands of the clock.

I continued reading vociferously, both fiction and non-fiction while maintaining my interest in literature and sports. I enjoyed debating on a variety of subjects, particularly current affairs, with my colleagues. A couple of them turned into friends, both in the bank and outside of it.

I was growing more and more confident. Nothing spectacular or noteworthy happened in the first six months, except for a few funny incidents in the bank that reflected the mood of bank employees during those days.

We had no calculators or computers. Everything was done manually. Typewriters were the only advanced devices in use.

I was first placed in the Remittance section of the bank and was asked to sit at the counter which issued demand drafts. About 400-500 drafts were issued daily, some of them typed and others handwritten.

For the first three days, I was learning, not just how to write demand drafts, but also how to prepare supporting debit/credit vouchers and send advices to corresponding branches on which the drafts were drawn.

Our bank timings were 10:15 a.m. to 5:45 p.m. I would leave sharp at 5:45 p.m. but often saw many of my colleagues still working. My officer had to work late nights to check and sign all the drafts completed by the clerks.

In the morning when I reached the office, two of my colleagues would already be at work.

On the fourth day, I asked a senior colleague if I could be of help. He simply responded, "It's up to you." I did not understand the reasoning behind that.

I turned to another senior colleague and asked how I could help him. He responded that he would speak to the officer. I was totally at a loss to understand why no one was accepting my offer to help, even more so because it was work for which I was already being paid by the bank.

That same afternoon, my officer asked me whether I would like to work overtime. I immediately responded that I wouldn't mind doing so. My father had advised me – "you should not refuse to work overtime if asked to and you will be paid for those extra hours."

I was asked to come early the next day at 8:30 a.m. The next day, I reached the bank at 8:15 a.m. None of my colleagues had arrived. I had no idea how to start the work.

After an hour, a senior colleague who saw me sitting around asked what I had done since I came to work.

"Nothing," I responded.

He showed me the drawer where the demand draft applications were stored and asked me to begin working on them if I arrived earlier than he did.

My work processing the drafts was interrupted at 10:15 a.m. when he asked me to stop working overtime and to start attending to customers.

It took a few days for me to fully understand the process. No matter how much actual extra time we worked, we were given two hours of daily overtime.

I was not happy.

One such morning, I came to the bank at 8:00 a.m. as I knew we had a backlog of more than 300 demand draft applications pending from the previous evening.

I began preparing demand drafts, vouchers and advices as fast as I could. My senior colleague came in at 9:30 a.m. and inquired how far I had reached.

I let him know that only 35 applications remained. He said "good" in a rather subdued tone as if it was not from his heart. I was puzzled as I thought I had worked well.

About 15 minutes later, my officer came to check on my progress. He was surprised and happy with my efficiency. He appreciated me, loud enough for others to hear. I was encouraged.

Again, the next day, we had to come early to finish about 250 pending demand draft applications.

This time I came in at 7:15 a.m. My officer was in at 9:00 a.m. and started checking and signing.

I enthusiastically told him, "Sir, I have just finished all of it."

My senior colleague came in at his usual time of 9:30 a.m. inquiring about the status of the work. My officer turned to my senior colleague and told him, "I appreciate this boy. For the first time since I joined this department, I will reach home early and have dinner with my wife and children."

I thanked him for the compliment.

My senior colleague did not comment, nor did he react.

But when our officer went for lunch, he said, "Look Vijay, if you want to cooperate with me, then it is okay, otherwise, take a transfer to some other department."

I was disappointed and shocked, maybe even hurt.

I told him, "Sir, I have tried my best to complete it fast, I will try to increase my speed."

He said, "No, no. You slow down, otherwise, we will lose our overtime."

I went home and briefed my father.

He asked me to continue working the way I was, taking care that my officer did not have any complaint against me.

This is when I also realized that officers were not eligible for overtime.

I continued working the same way to the utmost discomfort of my colleagues. They were grumbling to the officer about losing overtime. But our officer had also gotten used to leaving and coming to the bank on time, finishing the previous days' pending work during normal working hours.

One day, my officer called me and said, "See Vijay, both your colleagues are not happy with you. They are seniors and are also staff union representatives. I am just informing you, but as far as I am concerned, you are doing a good job. The staff union is powerful. No officer can afford to complain against its representatives."

I immediately sensed that I could not afford to spoil the relationship with my colleagues. Having understood the system of overtime, in the presence of my two colleagues, I suggested to my officer that if we received a certain number of demand drafts on a particular day, all three of us would get two hours of overtime, irrespective of who finishes the work and when. Everyone agreed.

I continued working my way. Not having family responsibilities, I would sometimes work an extra hour, so that none of us would need to come early the next day, but would still get our overtime.

I informed my father about my suggestion being accepted. He did not say anything, but he was not happy about getting overtime without working the extra hours.

My seniors had told me "Remember OT is Roti." Overtime is your bread and butter (and salary is savings).

I realized that humans by nature generally demand an immediate solution to a problem. Not even considering its complexity.

CHAPTER TEN

After about a month, I was fortunate to be selected to go to the staff training college for three months, with 100 other colleagues. The training came with its perks – breakfast, lunch, snacks. We had a gala time, and before we knew it, our training was complete.

Upon completion, I was placed in the Fixed Deposits department. Our head of department was Mr Mukesh Sharma, an ex-army officer, who had saved the life of a high ranking General who later became a Field Marshal. Mr Sharma was a good friend of my father. I soon became his blue-eyed boy.

As time passed by, I grew in confidence creating my own identity in the bank. I was also selected for the bank's 'B' cricket team. I played a few competitive tournaments like the inter-office '*Times of India* Cricket Tournament'. My performance was not great, but not too bad either, especially with the bat and behind the stumps. My performance was acknowledged by the captain and by my teammates.

Things were going well. I had a job and was able to play cricket which I loved.

Then, an event that changed the path of my life happened.

It was a cool morning on a mid-January day in 1968. I had taken the 7 a.m. train to the office. Many students were also travelling in the same compartment. Soon, they started arguing angrily on a trivial issue. Two groups were formed. I worried they would end up in a physical fight and moved away creating some distance from them.

Seeing the commotion, an elderly gentleman intervened and asked a question of them.

"Would you all have behaved in the same fashion if you had to earn and shoulder wider family responsibilities?"

One boy immediately retorted, "Uncle, we are all employed. We are pursuing our college education in the morning and go to work right after. We have a habit of arguing loudly. Anyway, thanks for your concern."

I moved closer to the boy sitting next to me. "What is the procedure of joining the morning college? What course are you pursuing?"

After confirming that I was also already employed, he said, "I am completing Arts and intend to pursue Economics. Generally, college classes are from 7 a.m. to 10 a.m. after which we go to our respective offices. We are late today as we have our monthly tests. Other days, we catch the 6 a.m. train."

I listened to him intently.

"All you need to produce is your certificate of employment to the college in which you wish to be enrolled. Morning or evening colleges are meant only for employed students."

I thanked him and now saw a potential path for me to complete my education, something I had thought would never be possible. It was a good idea to pursue. At least I would be called a graduate and would qualify for an early promotion. I could become an officer, go to the "For Officers Only" areas, dine in a separate canteen, and order tea over the phone. I would not have to do any clerical work, but only check and supervise work done by others. I would have the authority to sign off on cheques and drafts. All these from my office table with an officer's chair. My social status would go up.

It seemed like there were many privileges without any disadvantages. I felt a change in thinking would change my future behaviour. Both were interdependent and interconnected. I had dreamt up a positive future state and I now had a pathway to achieve it.

Engrossed in such thoughts, I reached the office.

CHAPTER ELEVEN

I discussed this option with a few senior colleagues. Most of them backed my thoughts and encouraged me to go ahead. Two of them even decided to join me.

Just then, I overheard two colleagues talking to one another. "Why does he have to do that?" "He can get whatever he wants in the bank. His father will do it for him."

This irked me to no end. I turned around, about to lose my temper, but held myself back just in time.

In a calm yet firm voice, I declared, "Friends, this is my vow – I will not seek promotion as long as my father is in the bank. I will apply for it only when he retires."

One of them apologised saying he was just joking. I told him, "As a matter of fact, you have cautioned me that some people are or may have been carrying such feelings. Thank you for this."

I kept up that promise, not just to prove it to others, but for myself too.

On the way back home in the evening, I deliberated with myself. If I pursued further studies, it would mean an extra financial burden on the family. Our financial position had not improved. After dinner, I talked to my father.

"*Bha*, I want to study further."

"What do you want to study?"

"B.A."

"Instead, why can't you do CAIIB?"

"I will do it once I complete B.A."

"What would the fees be?"

"Rs.120 a year."

"Will you be able to do it seriously?"

"I am sure I will be able to. This degree will help me in my career."

"OK, go ahead."

And that was it. Just like that, I had permission to pursue my studies. I was relieved and excited.

It was June 1968. I collected my certificate of employment from the bank and went to the college which was a 10 to 15-minute walk from my office.

I was easily admitted to an Arts course and thus began the second innings of my student life.

The first few days of college were a bit tough. I had to wake up at 5 a.m., catch the 5:50 a.m. train and reach college by 6:50 a.m. just in time for the morning 7 a.m. classes. At 10 a.m. I had to rush to the office before 10:15 a.m. by which time all staff members were required to be at their desks. At 3:30 p.m., I had to leave for cricket net practice, after which I had to catch the 6 p.m. train to reach home by 6:30 p.m.

I was completely exhausted and it was becoming a challenge to sustain this lifestyle. I wondered what adjustments need to be made, but no solutions were obvious.

As luck would have it, I found a solution through an unpleasant incident.

We were to play a friendly cricket match on a Sunday. One of our players, a very good friend of the captain, did not report on time for the match. Yet, the captain in the hope that he would show up, included his name in the playing eleven, in the face of a protest from all other players including me (if only we had cell phones in those days). I was disappointed to be named the 12th man, a position known for carrying water during the drinks break or substituting as a fielder for an injured player. Hardly a desirable role. We lost that match by just one run. Immediately after the match, I informed our captain that I would like to withdraw from the bank's team and would not join net practice from the next day onwards. He apologised and tried to persuade me to stay, but I did not budge.

Not having to go for cricket practice gave me some relief from becoming exhausted at the end of the day. Was this the real reason for my not budging? Perhaps yes. Most decisions in life are normally determined by circumstances.

Even though the morning college was strictly meant for employed students, I found that more than half the students used fake employment certificates. After class, they would hang out in the college the whole day.

CHAPTER TWELVE

There was hardly any scope to make new friends in college because of my hectic schedule. Sometimes, I would get the opportunity to interact with my classmates.

Being a sociable person, I missed not having friends and thought of ways to go about making some.

One day, a professor, Bharat Mehta, announced in class that the Gujarati Sahitya Mandal (Gujarati Cultural Association) would be holding elections for office bearers after three weeks. Those who wanted to contest could do so.

After class, I expressed my interest in contesting. Professor Mehta looked at me, smiled sarcastically, and in an almost equally sarcastic tone, said, "From the 12 divisions, 24 members will be voting. And out of those, 22 would be from day college and only two, including you from morning college. Do you know anyone? Rather, does anyone know you? Will anyone vote for you?"

I responded that I wanted to contest for the post of Joint Secretary.

He asked me the reason for my interest.

I explained, "Sir, since my childhood, I have taken on a leadership role in the school, college, and community activities. Even now, I am a class representative. I will not be disappointed if I lose the election. On the contrary, I will have the satisfaction of at least having tried. And in the bargain, make some friends."

He looked at me in disbelief. After a brief pause, he asked me to first pay the fees to become a member of the Association and then fill out the election form.

I asked him if I would get a chance to address the voters as I hardly had any time to campaign actively.

He explained that the procedure was that I would get 15 days to campaign, and on election day before voting began, all candidates would get an opportunity to address the voters. He cautioned me to think twice, reminding me that never in the history of the Association, had a morning college student been elected. No morning college student had ever even contested.

I filled out the form and took a day's casual leave to campaign. My opponent was Anita Shah, three years my senior. As I established individual contact with eligible voters, I learnt that she was from a rich family. She was a favourite of the professor who served as the ex-officio chairman of the Association. She appeared over-confident. I sensed that the general feeling of the voters was that she was a bit arrogant given she had been elected unopposed for the last three years.

It was good to see her face an election this time around. While no one was too vocal about this, I sensed an undertone in their silence. I could hear their unspoken words. This gave me confidence and comfort.

I knew that it was a daunting task. There was a contest for every post – President, Vice President, Secretary, Joint Secretary, Treasurer, and six other Committee Members.

Three days before the election, Professor Mehta called me to the staff room. He had an eagle eye on the campaign and asked, "Vijay, today is the last day for withdrawing nominations. What have you decided?"

I was not surprised. Anita was his preferred candidate.

"Sir, since an election will be held for all other posts, let there also be an election for the post of Joint Secretary."

Ever since the elections were announced, the voters were divided into two camps, with each camp equally confident of their support. I decided not to take sides and join a camp. It was almost certain that my vote would be decisive. So, I was wooed by both camps and was repeatedly approached for my support. Contesting candidates would come to the college before 7:00 a.m. to talk to me and would wait for me to come out at 10:00 a.m., walk with me to the bank and talk to me to impress me to vote for them.

I observed that my opponent was not bothering to campaign at all. It was almost as if she thought she was guaranteed to win. The professor, indirectly campaigning on her behalf, was asking voters to vote for her. I was also prepared for the outcome. I was not in a position to campaign because of my work. However, I was friendly with everyone, careful to not choose sides. By now, all the voters knew me, if not by face, at least by name. I was known as the candidate contesting against another candidate whose victory was a foregone conclusion.

Well, election day arrived.

All 24 of us gathered in a classroom. Professor Mehta provided a gist of activities of the Association since its inception and then asked us to vote for candidates who we thought would be best able to constructively contribute to the activities of the Association. Contesting presidents, vice presidents and secretaries spoke about themselves and their skills and gave enough reasons why everyone should vote for them.

It was then the turn of the contesting joint secretaries.

Anita was invited to speak first. She spoke from her seat, not bothering to even come to the stage. She announced, "I don't want to tell anyone anything about me, as everyone knows me." She glanced at me and gave me a victorious smile.

I was not looking at her, instead, I looked around to see how others were reacting. I sensed that almost everyone had expressions on their faces rejecting her attitude. Here was a candidate who had not even bothered to get up from her seat. Seeing this, I grew in confidence. This wasn't the first time I would be appearing on stage. I had won a school elocution competition a few years ago, and on many other occasions managed many events. I was also a prefect from third to eleventh grade and a class representative in college too.

I was not short on confidence, but in this situation, I had to address an unknown audience. While the outcome seemed almost pre-decided, in those few seconds, I resolved to do my best to send my message across.

I had not prepared a speech but had a good idea about the message I wanted to convey. The substance was in place, the words needed discovering. I heard one of the candidates, Sachin Parekh, speak. He was a well-known Gujarati stage artist. He was totally at ease when he spoke. That inspired me to also be at ease.

I remembered telling other candidates when they individually approached me to vote for them, that both sides were equal for me, but I had only one vote, so wait and see what happens. Without taking anyone's side, I did not reveal my preference keeping my choice in suspense. That stand probably helped me, forcing the other voters to talk to and about me.

When it was my turn, I stood up. Sachin wished me the best of luck. He was loud and perhaps wanted to send a message to his opponent that I was with him. I smiled at him and immediately smiled at his opponent too. Both of them gave me a warm thank you smile. When

I was on stage, I looked around and continued smiling, trying to connect personally with each individual.

I started speaking. "Our beloved professor, outgoing office bearers and committee members of the Gujarati Sahitya Mandal. We often hear that an election is the soul of any democracy, but how about we leave the slogans for the politicians? Is it appropriate in our student years to fight elections in the college? We are likely to be associated with it for a maximum of four years. Why is it necessary to indulge in a power struggle? To satisfy an individual ego? Or to settle personal scores with someone? I am sure you will be tempted to ask me, and rightly so, why then did I choose to fight the election? Why don't you announce right now that you do not want to fight the election and withdraw from the contest? Am I right?" I paused here for a few seconds. There was pin-drop silence in the room.

I could see the anticipation in the room wondering what I was going to say next. Their eagerness was obvious including that of the professor.

I went on, "Your questions, as I am guessing, are appropriate and your likely reaction are also justifiable. But, until we successfully abolish the election process from all educational institutions, unfortunately, we have to honour the existing process. And that is why friends, I have to request you to give your vote to me. Whether I earn it or not, with all seriousness I am announcing that I will take the lead, with all your support, to abolish the election process from colleges. We will take a step in the direction of selection rather than election under the supervision of the professor in charge. We will all move on and leave the college in three to four years, but our professor will be there till he retires. And therefore, there is no one else more deserving to select who serves on the Association. Thank you."

As I descended from the stage, I heard loud and continuous applause, in which even the professor joined in.

I went to my seat and took a while to cool down. The voting started. It would not take too long to complete.

When done, the two camps started congratulating and thanking their camp members. Each of them felt that I had voted in their favour and thanked me too. I just smiled at them. After all, I had just one vote.

The counting began and wouldn't take long to finish. In the meantime, we were enjoying tea, coffee, and snacks.

Soon, Professor Mehta came on stage to announce the results.

"Dear students, each year, we hold the elections of the Gujarati Sahitya Mandal of our college. One team always wins and one team loses. Before I continue,

I want to inform you that for one of the posts, I will announce the results at the end. That is for the post of Joint Secretary. I am not indicating anything, but for the last three years, this post was won unopposed. This time, it was contested."

He started announcing results from the post of the President down to the Committee Members, skipping announcing results for the post of Joint Secretary. Before he could announce the result for the post of Joint Secretary, both the presidential candidates rushed to me to say that I had not voted for them. Calmly, I told them that it was strange that both the winner and the loser were accusing me of not having voted for them. Because the difference was only two votes, it meant that each of them had counted the number of votes they expected to get. "Do you agree that I have given my vote to one of you? Why are you both not trying to find who cross-voted from your camp?" Before they could respond, the professor asked them to go back to their respective seats.

He continued, "Friends, you know that both the candidates for the post of Joint Secretary did not belong to any group. I expect both the candidates and all of you to accept the results in the true spirit, and work to enhance the image of our Association in the college. I solicit everyone's cooperation. Out of the two candidates, one has been elected unopposed for the last three years and for the first time, is facing an election. The other candidate is from the morning college. I wondered how he must have campaigned or whether he campaigned at all. Except, he got an opportunity to address all of you just before the voting began. I admire his confidence. I now request both the candidates to come on stage."

Everyone was eagerly awaiting the outcome. We both went on stage. I was a bit nervous but prepared to accept whatever the result was. I somehow managed to maintain a neutral expression on my face.

Professor Mehta asked, "Do you both want me to announce only the result of who won and lost, or the result with the number of votes polled?"

I immediately said that I was fine either way. Some voices from the audience asked for only the result. Others asked for results of the number of votes polled.

My opponent, Anita said, "No sir, you must announce who got how many votes."

"Okay", he said, "The result is 22-2. Vijay has 22, and Anita has 2."

She was surprised, hesitatingly congratulated me and quickly walked out.

After a moment of complete silence, everyone started congratulating me. Professor Mehta said, "Well done, I did not expect this."

I felt a sense of deep satisfaction. This event had increased my self-confidence. This self-confidence proved to be one of my most trusted assets for years to come. I learnt that, in both good times and difficult situations, sincere and honest efforts are bound to bring incredible results.

CHAPTER THIRTEEN

My involvement with my college Association coincided with an unanticipated movement in our community to revive the almost defunct Youth Association. I became a member of the committee managing the Youth Association. A typical committee member was 40 years old, so I was the youngest. I was enthusiastic following my success in the college cultural association election.

At the first official meeting, I proposed organizing a cultural variety entertainment programme with artists selected only from the community. I also suggested making this a fundraising event by way of advertisements to be published in a souvenir.

Our community is small and tightly knit. Most of our elders came to India around the time of the partition and settled in Mumbai and lived in the same neighbourhood. At the same time, however, the younger generation in the community was not connected, at least not in the way our elders were.

Organizing a cultural event would be a great opportunity to connect the youth in the community. It would also allow us to get involved in social work and provide a platform to showcase our talents. It would help increase everyone's confidence in participating in such events in the future. This idea was well received by the committee members. With the help of the senior members of the committee, we created a blueprint for the event.

I could sense an all-around enthusiasm in the community as it would be the first such event of its kind. Since almost all of us were working professionals or students, practice sessions were possible only in the evening, typically between 6 p.m. and 9 p.m. We practised in the south Bombay premises of a member of our community, who generously allowed us to use his space. Participants came from all over the city, including the suburbs. To alleviate concerns of parents of girls and boys travelling late at night, we made arrangements to drop them home, with one of us accompanying them.

I used to wake up at 4:30 a.m., go to college, then office and practice session by 6 p.m. After practice, we shared the responsibility of dropping the boys and girls home. So, it was usually midnight by the time I got home. It was tiring, but our enthusiasm to make the event a grand success kept us going.

Not to forget, we also had to try to solicit advertisements for our souvenir. Everyone put in their best efforts. I was assigned to a team of our community's leading businessmen. I took a leave of 15 days from the bank. We would meet after my college hours and visit our contacts seeking funds. In the evening, they would attend to their business and I would head for the practice session.

As if all of this was not sufficient, I was to perform a solo one-act play written by me. I also had the sole responsibility of getting the souvenir printed – everything from content to proof checking to finalizing the layout. The last month was hectic, and yet I was enjoying it. One good thing at this time was that I came into contact with people of my age, many of whom I had never met before. One such introduction was significant.

One evening, before our practice began, we were eating street food. I saw a girl accompany my elder sister for practice. I casually asked my sister who she was. She said, "Her name is Jaya, daughter of Mr Bhagwandas Kesaria. She is my student and my neighbour." I acknowledged her reply and said hello to Jaya. She just smiled and nodded.

In addition to the entertainment programme, we also decided to give prizes to bright students of the community, as a means of encouragement. We also decided to honour someone as the community's first social worker. An individual who contributed to the upliftment of the community and was well recognized in his or her field would be selected. I had to buy the prizes and look after almost every arrangement including stage management and dresses for artists.

We rented an auditorium at one of South Bombay's leading colleges to hold the function. This was the first time that many, actually almost 99.9%, of the artists were performing in an auditorium.

The D-Day arrived. I was not nervous, but anxious. I heard murmurs of my praise. That made me happy. All the performers gave their one hundred per cent. The solo and group dances, both traditional and modern, were appreciated.

The honour of being the first leading social worker of the community went to my father. He was chosen by the elders. When introducing his achievements, the President of the Association spoke about his interests, his position in the bank, and his flair for writing as a contributor to a weekly in Karachi, where we lived pre-partition.

He continued, "Mr Thariani is instrumental in finding employment for many members of our community." He started reading the names of the individuals my father had helped. When the speaker reached the third or fourth name from a long list, my father stopped him and requested him to not announce any more names.

My father, who always earned but never demanded respect, said, "I have only done the job of introducing them to management. All of them got the job because of their own merits, qualifications, performance in the written tests and interviews. I have not obliged anyone. Therefore, I request you to please not read the names."

Thunderous applause broke out; a befitting reaction. My father was awarded a certificate and a medal. Many students got prizes for their academic achievements in different subjects. One such recipient was my elder sister's student and neighbour. Yes, Jaya!

CHAPTER FOURTEEN

It was a Sunday, the day after the function. All conversations revolved around it – who was good, outstanding, which item was the best, whose performance was the best, and so on.

Suddenly my father walked up to me, patted me on the back, and said, "Well done." He went on to offer some sage advice, "Remember Vijay, today you are getting all praises, but sometimes you may get brickbats. If you want to do social work, you should wear a bulletproof jacket all the time." I remember his golden advice even today. Therefore, if I hear some criticism for my work today, I am easily able to ignore it.

My eldest sister and brother-in-law joined us for lunch that afternoon. After lunch, we continued to talk about the function. Out of the blue, my sister said, "How about we think of getting Vijay engaged?" My parents looked at me.

I protested, "I am still young, only 21 years old and still studying." My brother-in-law suggested I get engaged now and the wedding could take place after graduation. Without waiting for my reaction, my sister said they had a girl in mind for me. My mother asked whose daughter she was.

"She is the daughter of Mr Bhagwandas Kesaria, our neighbour. She is a very good, cultured and bright girl. We have watched her grow."

I did not react but was anxious to see what happened next. I thought to myself, "Oh, she is the girl I was introduced to by my sister." At that moment, a thought crossed my mind, "Well, maybe she could be the one…"

My parents looked at me, expecting me to say yes. In those days, it was not possible to argue with parents. We had to read the language of their eyes. And I could read theirs. My response was the same as when my father asked whether I wanted to work, "As you feel appropriate."

Our engagement ceremony was a simple one. As was the norm, my father accepted one rupee and 25 paise as a token of confirmation of the relationship. Jaya and I touched the feet of our elders. And that was it. I thought to myself – I am no longer a boy. I have now become a man and have to behave more maturely, more responsibly.

This reminded me of an incident that took place during the wedding of a friend's brother. I distinctly remember that two days before the wedding, we had to visit the bride's house to deliver a formal wedding invitation from the groom's family to the bride's, a tradition to reconfirm the wedding date.

About 20 of us had gone to the bride's house. As we were going up the stairs of the house, my friend stopped us. He asked us to wait for the bride's family to come down, greet us, and invite us to their house. In the meantime, my friend started singing wedding songs. The message went up and they came down to greet us.

Both families were singing wedding songs with joy. They were trying to outdo each other, sometimes using sarcastic and sharp language. I realized it was friendly banter, the purpose of which was not to hurt sentiments but enjoyment.

This same situation took place at another wedding. In that case, however, for many years the couple carried a feeling that my friend was trying to obstruct the wedding. Their attitude towards him was always one of disdain. My friend felt bad about this.

I did not think too deeply at that time, but I now realize that every community and every society has its customs, which must be respected and followed. While we strive to keep pace with changing times, traditional values must be protected.

My friend admitted his mistake and resolved that in the future he would never suggest anything that would hurt the sentiments of others.

Back to my engagement. If you ask me today, I would say that engagement is a golden period in one's life. No, I am not going to write even a single incident of that phase as I believe it is not a matter of describing, but of experiencing.

CHAPTER FIFTEEN

My college did not offer a combination of literature and philosophy subjects, which I was interested in. So, I enrolled in another college, also at an equal distance to my office as my existing college. I was still in Junior B.A. and had one more year to graduate.

Before I left college, I experienced an incident that taught me a lot.

Professor Mukesh Wadhwa was the head of the History Department. It was said that he had read, cover to cover, every history book available in the college library. He had authored a few books on history.

During our quarterly exams, in response to a particular question, I referenced Chapter XI in a book written by a particular author.

Professor Wadhwa was in the habit of going through the answer sheets of students who received the highest marks, as well as of those that scored the lowest. This was likely because he wanted to make sure that there was no favouritism on the part of the junior examiner to someone they knew or any vengeance towards someone they did not like.

Professor Wadhwa was not only the head of the Department of History but also the Chief Moderator of History at the University. I scored 48 marks out of 50 in the exam. The examiner Mr Sunil Deshpande was lavish with his praise in class. I was naturally very happy. A few days later, the examiner and I were summoned by Professor Wadhwa to his chamber. He welcomed us, asked us to have a seat, and offered us tea. After congratulating me, he turned to Mr Deshpande and asked, "Professor, I have seen Vijay's answers. What did you like best in his answers?"

Mr Deshpande replied, "Sir, I liked that his answers were to the point and also the language."

Professor Wadhwa retorted, "Mr Deshpande, history deals with facts and not the fluency of language."

Professor Deshpande was perplexed. He was asked to leave. As soon as he left, Professor Wadhwa turned to me and asked, "Tell me Vijay, I do not recall a quote you referenced in Chapter XI of the book you referred to in your answer. I don't remember reading it in the book. Are you sure it is from this book?"

For a moment, I was taken aback. I told him, "Sir, while stating the reference, I was sure about it, however, after submitting the answer sheet, I had a doubt. Because I was unsure of the source of the quote, I went to the library and found that the quote was not in the book that I mentioned. Nervously, I tried to recall what I had written, when I remembered another book written by the same author. I was relieved and happy to find the quote in Chapter XI of that book."

I admitted my mistake.

He smiled, got up from his chair, and patted me on the back. He said, "I appreciate you admitting your mistake. I am glad that you did not lie. But in the future, you need to be 100% sure of what you write, particularly when you give a reference in writing or when you speak about someone having said or referred to something."

I apologized and thanked him and have been following his advice ever since.

CHAPTER SIXTEEN

Unlike my previous college, in my new one, most fellow students were professionally employed. Only about 15 of us had chosen Gujarati literature. The Philosophy class, taught by Professor Janak Divecha, had about twice that number.

Our textbook was *My Experiments with Truth* by Mahatma Gandhi. Professor Divecha was a true Gandhian. He would explain the various chapters and topics discussed in the book, with passion and a complete understanding of the subject.

One day, he was describing and explaining an incident from the book, where Gandhiji was forcefully dragging Kasturba, his wife, outside the house. Sitting in the first row, I was lost in thought, perhaps not listening to the professor. He noticed this and called out 'Vijay!' He had seen through my expressions, or the lack of them, that I was inattentive and not concentrating on what he was teaching.

"What are you thinking?" he asked.

"Sorry Sir, I was lost in thoughts," I replied.

"What thoughts?" he asked

I told him that I would like to meet him after class and share my thoughts with him.

He was upset by my inattentiveness, and said, "Tell me what and now. You have already disturbed me."

"Sir, I will come to you after the class and tell you what I was preoccupied with," I argued.

He insisted, still very angry, and said that it was an order. "Tell me here and just now."

I knew I was his favourite student, but looking at his stony glance and insistence, I gathered courage and said, "Sir, while you were appreciating Gandhiji's frank admission of his misbehaviour with Kasturba and explaining how great he was, a question arose in my mind. I thought when Gandhiji was writing *My Experiments with Truth*, people were already worshipping him. He openly admitted his weaknesses and wrongdoings. This was his greatness. I was wondering how he was able to muster up the courage to do so. What could be the reason?"

Hearing this, Professor Divecha's face turned red with anger.

I continued, "So, I feel, when Gandhiji himself exposed his weaknesses and wrongdoings, his image and status in society was well-established. If any of us regular people admit to somethings similar, even if done in our younger days, say stealing or engaging in immoral acts or physically abusing our wives what would society say about us? I am sure society would call us all possible names, instead of appreciating our frankness as they did in the case of Gandhiji. Why? Because we do not enjoy the status Gandhiji enjoyed. Sir, I am sorry, but these thoughts were running through my mind."

Professor Divecha was now truly shaking with anger.

He shouted, "How can you even think about Gandhiji in this manner? Villains like you should be crushed under the feet of an elephant." He rushed out of the class.

I was stunned and scared. Why did I say this? Our half-yearly exams were coming up. Was I going to fail the class? Would I need to repeat a year? These thoughts ran through my mind. My fellow students came to me and agreed that I was right. They thought that the professor should have answered my question. I thanked everyone and said, "I feel we are young. Professor Divecha is experienced. Either my representation was wrong or I was wrong in my interpretation. I will close this chapter here and seek his pardon tomorrow." My fellow students started murmuring among themselves and I even heard somebody saying that I was a coward.

For the entire day, I was disturbed by this incident. The more I thought, the more I resolved to seek his pardon as I could not afford to waste an academic year.

I was not able to sleep that night. The next morning, I reached college at 6:30 a.m. and inquired after Professor Divecha. The peon said that he had not come in yet. I went to class in time for his 7 a.m. lecture. All the students were there even before I entered the class. Everyone was anxious to know the fallout of yesterday's outburst. Though no one said anything, I sensed their support for me.

However, I could not help thinking about whether I would be expelled or failed. There was pin-drop silence. 7, 7:05, 7:10, 7:15 – Professor Divecha did not turn up. Every passing minute felt like an hour.

Finally, at 7:15 a.m. the peon came to the class and asked me to see the professor. I went to his office and stood in front of him, face down.

He coldly said, "Sit."

I followed his command mechanically. He said, "Vijay, I was not able to sleep last night." I interrupted him, "Sir, I'm very sorry. Please forgive me."

I looked at his face. His eyes were red.

He held my hand and continued, "For the entire night, I was thinking about your question. I concluded in the morning that it was most appropriate, and there was nothing wrong with it. I will answer it in class. Go back and inform everyone that I will come at 8 AM. And yes, you need not feel sorry, I am sorry."

My eyes filled with tears. In an emotional voice, I said, "Thank you Sir" and ran out of the staff room. I wiped my eyes. Everyone asked me what had happened. I said, "Nothing. Sir will take the class at 8 a.m."

My classmates began to speculate, their earlier assurances of support, seemingly evaporating in the air.

At exactly 8 a.m. Divecha Sir entered the class. There was complete silence.

He asked, "Friends how many of you are with Vijay?"

No one said a word. After about a minute, he said, "After contemplating his question the whole night, I concluded that it was appropriate and my instant reaction was uncalled for. I was wrong. For this, I have already apologized to him and am saying this again in front of you all – Vijay, I am sorry."

This time, I couldn't hold back my tears. I got up from my seat and touched his feet and said, "Sir, today you are more than Gandhiji to me. Bless me."

He hugged me. I could feel his tears on my cheeks.

From this incident, it was clear to me that that one should not feel ashamed to admit one's mistake in front of all concerned. The whole class, including Professor Divecha, was silent for more than five minutes. That day, for the first time, I fully understood the power of silence.

CHAPTER SEVENTEEN

Despite not wanting to do so, I am unable to resist the temptation to compare Professor Divecha and Professor Mehta.

After the elections of the Gujarati Cultural Association, Professor Mehta developed a soft corner for me and trusted my abilities to organize cultural events in college. And I did not disappoint him. One Friday he asked me to come to a specific hotel.

"So, what is the agenda?" I inquired.

All he said was, "Come tomorrow, you will not regret it. Plus, if you come, I will be very happy."

I reached the venue at the appointed time the next day. There were about 12 other youngsters already there. I did not recognize any of them. Professor Mehta welcomed us all and said, "Once a month I call some youngsters to read out poems written by them." He introduced me to the other participants. One after the other they recited their poems. I was the only one left. Suddenly, he invited me to recite any poem that I had written. I was not prepared. I asked him to excuse me.

He said, "No, I know you write poetry."

I replied, "That is only for my pleasure, Sir. And my diary is at home."

He insisted, "Vijay, nothing doing, you have to recite at least a few lines. Whatever you remember."

I nervously looked outside the window, where I saw a lemonade seller. Somehow, I managed to make up a poem about him and recited four or five lines. Amidst clapping, Professor Mehta said, "Very good."

I felt encouraged. The next day, I took the poetry collection in my diary and requested him to give his opinion and suggestions. He agreed and took the diary. After a week or two, he returned it to me, saying – "Good effort. Keep it up!" I was encouraged.

A few weeks after I changed colleges, I came to know that Professor Mehta's new poetry collection had been published. I picked up a copy from the stands. While reading, I could not believe that in many of his poems, the central idea was based on work done by me, and in certain cases, many verses were reproduced without any change. I was angry and frustrated. I tore off my precious work thinking who would believe that it was my original work if it was already published by a renowned professor.

It was interesting to compare the two lessons I learned. Professor Divecha's message was – 'Do not hesitate to admit your mistake there is nothing to be ashamed about.' While Professor Mehta's message was – 'Be opportunistic whenever possible.'

I have followed the advice of Professor Divecha all my life and have rejected the lesson I learned from Professor Mehta.

CHAPTER EIGHTEEN

The date of our wedding was finally decided, with my elder sister's wedding fixed for the day before, and Jaya's sister's wedding fixed for the same time as ours. Everyone was happy. But I could see two images on the faces of my family members. One was that of happiness and the other of stress about the wedding expenses. How would we meet such expenses with a limited family income?

I hesitantly asked my father, "How we will meet these expenses?"

He said, "It will be arranged. You don't worry."

To this day, I am not aware of how he managed it. My elder sister's wedding was celebrated with appropriate fanfare and it did justice to the occasion. For my wedding the next day, the programme, which started in the early evening, was something as follows:

Reach venue at 5 p.m.

Hastmelap 6 p.m.

Reception 7 p.m. to 9 p.m.

After 10 p.m., the wedding ceremony based on sacred rituals. It would end the next morning at around 2 a.m.

In the morning hours, Jaya's younger brothers' sacred thread ceremony took place. I was not allowed to attend that function, thanks to the practice that the groom cannot go to his in-law's house on the day of his wedding.

I was alone at home, while everyone else went to the thread ceremony and had lunch too. As I waited, my friends invited me to play a one-inning softball cricket match. With no one there to stop me, I, the groom, went to play a cricket match on my wedding day. After the match, I realized I was hungry. So I ordered a *sada dosa* from a South Indian restaurant for 25 paise. After about an hour, everyone returned from the thread ceremony function and got busy preparing for my wedding function that evening. Amidst all the excitement, no one even bothered to ask what I was up to and I too got busy preparing for that evening.

We had a joint reception with Jaya's sister. My wish to not have live music during the reception was overruled. I reasoned that because the stage for the music party would be in the opposite direction of our reception stage we might end up seeing the back of our guests who would likely be more interested in enjoying live music. No one was convinced and went ahead with the plans. Playing live music at wedding receptions was the trend in those days. My fears came true. It was quite funny to see guests come up on stage, greet us, step down, then select their seats and turn in the opposite direction to watch the band. Well, at least they were entertained and had a good time.

The wedding was done. A small ceremony was performed the day after, and it was time to go for our honeymoon to Kashmir – considered to be heaven on earth. But travelling there was going to be rather expensive. I knew that in advance. I had calculated the costs and accordingly made arrangements. We travelled by train in First Class, made available by my employer under the Leave Fare Concession policy which I was eligible for.

Through the Jammu and Kashmir (J&K) Tourism Office, I booked Hotel Badshah, a government-run hotel, in Srinagar, the capital city of J&K. It cost us just Rs. 30 per day, about 75% cheaper than other hotels with similar facilities. I had also booked daily bus tickets for Sonmarg, Yusmarg, Wular Lake, Mughal Gardens, Gulmarg, and Pahalgam. We would leave in the morning and come back in the evening to the hotel. In Pahalgam, we decided to spend a night. The daily bus fare was Rs. 30 per head. On the way back, we decided to spend two days in Delhi. The total cost of our honeymoon was therefore estimated to be Rs. 2,200.

Expense details:

Train fare – paid by the employer

The hotel bill for eight days (prepaid) – Rs. 240

Bus fare (prepaid) – Rs. 360

One night stay at Pahalgam – Rs. 60

Dinner for the entire stay – Rs. 240

Breakfast – included in the hotel tariff

Stay in Delhi and shopping – Rs. 1,000

Miscellaneous – Rs. 300

Total expenses – Rs. 2,200

I had made these arrangements two months earlier. I funded part of my trip by taking a small loan from a Diwali Fund – a fund created by colleagues contributing a certain monthly amount to it and then distributed to participants at the time of the festival. Interest earned on loans taken by a participant as well as interest on monthly contributions was parked with the bank in a separate account.

The remaining amount was arranged by utilizing Rs. 800 from the 'covers', cash given in sealed envelopes at the reception by wedding guests as gifts, and Rs. 500 from our family pool.

CHAPTER NINETEEN

With Rs. 1,600 in hand, we embarked on a journey to see and feel heaven on Earth.

Let me repeat that the engagement period cannot be described – it has to be experienced. Similarly, no words are enough to describe married life, but one has to experience this journey of togetherness.

In those days, you could get to Kashmir by train with the service up to Pathankot, about 350 km from Srinagar. A 14 to16 hour journey by bus would take you to Srinagar. I informed Jaya of our financial situation and about how much cash we had with us for a trip of 14 days including two nights in Delhi. She was the daughter of a jeweller, so I was not sure how she would take it and what she would think. But it was important to give her a clear financial picture of our honeymoon.

Immediately after I shared this with her, she said, "No problem, we will see that we complete our tour in the best possible manner with whatever we have in hand. Do not worry."

I sighed with relief and thanked God for my lovely and understanding better half. At that moment, I resolved that I must endeavour to see that she always remained my better half rather than me becoming her better half.

Before leaving Bombay, I had purchased a camera for Rs. 20, the kind that took postal stamp-sized black and white photos. From Pathankot, I bought a pocket transistor, a modest way to keep us entertained. By the time our train reached Pathankot, the last direct bus for Srinagar had left. We had an option to take a bus to Batod, a small town on the way to Srinagar, and stay the night there. Alternatively, we could stay overnight in Pathankot and take the first direct bus in the morning to Srinagar.

Communicating with our families to seek their opinion was hard as there were no direct phone lines. We could not afford the cost and time involved with placing a 'trunk call', which meant contacting an operator in an exchange who would then attempt to contact our families and then connect the two sides. We had taken a few postcards which we used to communicate with our families.

We decided to stay in Pathankot.

The next day, we got to Srinagar. I cannot resist narrating a small incident. It was my first independent trip with my wife. Bed tea and breakfast were included in our package with Badshah Hotel. I had never stayed in a big hotel until now, so I was nervous about etiquette. Someone knocked on the door at 4 a.m. I opened the door and encountered a well-dressed waiter. He came in and placed a tray with the tea on the side table. After waiting for a brief while, he left without uttering a word. We later realized that he was expecting a tip for the service rendered. We did not know that such a protocol existed, and even if we did, we could not have afforded any extra expense.

We dressed up and headed to the dining room for the complimentary breakfast. The waiter asked us what we would like to order. We asked him what our choices were. "Corn flakes, cutlets or omelette, tea, and coffee."

Being a vegetarian, I told him to bring anything except an omelette. After a while, he returned with a tray of corn flakes, a pot of milk, sugar, cutlets, and hot water. We had no idea what cornflakes were, had never even seen it and wondered how to eat it. We had never tried anything beyond *idli, dosa, bhel* and *roti*, so this was very western to us. The waiter, who was watching us from a distance realized our confusion and rightly understood our dilemma. He came to us and said, "Sir, this is corn flakes. Pour some milk on it and sugar to your taste. You will enjoy it."

I asked him if he could help us. He served us and we thanked him.

CHAPTER TWENTY

Our day trips were exciting. To describe our excitement about the beauty of Kashmir will require me to charge the power of imagination to its fullest and make it infinite. Only then will I be able to justify a description of our out-of-this-world Kashmir experience suitably. No poet or writer can claim that their poetry or article describing the beauty of Kashmir is ultimate. The moment after writing the poem and thinking it is the best depiction of Kashmir when the poem is re-read, it is inevitable they feel something is lacking. Maybe this is why Amir Khusrau, the noted 13th-century poet and scholar, described the beauty of Kashmir in the Farsi couplet as, *"Agar firdaus bar roo-e zameen ast, Hameen ast-o hameen ast-o hameen ast"*. Or "If there is a paradise on Earth, it is this, it is this, it is this." But are even these words the ultimate description of the beauty of Kashmir? I don't think so.

All that I can say is that I had just experienced what poets had struggled to convey. I will attempt, however, to share with you an unforgettable experience in Pahalgam, where nature was most kind to give us a glimpse of the rarest of rare scenes from its treasure.

Before I take you there, let me take a moment to share what happened when we were checking out of the hotel. The waiter who taught us to eat corn flakes with milk came to us with the hope of receiving a good tip. Every rupee was precious and valuable to us. Every saved rupee would ensure our return to Bombay. However, we gave him a small tip. The disbelief on his face was visible. He was pleasantly surprised. I told him, "When we return from Pahalgam, we will meet again." I can never forget the expressions on his face. At that time, we resolved that if we ever visited Kashmir again, we would stay in the same hotel. And God willing, if we still find him there, then we can amply compensate him for what we could not do that day.

Both of us, helpless as we were, felt guilty until we were halfway to Pahalgam. We reached at around 1 p.m. and checked into our hotel. After a short rest, we stepped out at around 4 p.m.

The surroundings were serene and breathtaking. We could hear the soothing, relaxing burble of the stream. Babbles, ripples, and trickles of streams all around us sang in a chorus. We walked a good distance to reach a small strip mall with about five to six shops. The soothing sound of nature's music thinned down. It became bright and sunny.

As we were window shopping, the weather changed. In a split second, there was thunder and lightning. Before we knew it, we were in the midst of a hail storm. Having never seen something like this before, we took it as another gift from nature. We dashed for shelter under the roof of a photography shop, which was closed at that time of the day. The temperature dipped. We were shivering. As we wondered whether to head out and seek shelter elsewhere, the door of the shop opened. We turned around and saw an elderly lady coming out. She said in a concerned tone, *"Arre, aapne koi garam kapde nahi pehne. Yeh Pahalgam ki thand hai baccho. Chati mein ghus gai to pareshan ho jaoge."* ("What! How come you have not worn any warm clothes in this weather? Children, if this cold of Pahalgam gets into your body, your health will suffer"). She forced us inside, her kindness on full display. A few minutes later when the hailstorm stopped, we thanked her and left.

At that moment, I realized that I had organized a trip to Kashmir without any woollens. How ignorant and foolish of me. Perhaps that is why, from then on, Jaya took charge of the packing for all our trips.

Given our limited budget, we were not in a position to buy any warm clothes there. Still cold, we started walking back to the hotel. As luck would have it, it became dark and started raining. This time, we took shelter under the roof of another shop. Opposite it was a hillock. We were amazed to see that though it was raining all around, the centre of the hillock was dry. The sun shone brightly on the peak. It was surreal, unbelievable. Everything appeared to be divine. Heaven and Earth surely coexisted here.

We ate a quick dinner at a street food joint. By the time we got to the hotel, it was late, dark, and extremely cold. We asked for extra blankets, but there were none available as the other guests had already taken them. Our room had no heater. We were not able to sleep. In the middle of the night, to survive the cold, I put on my suit, tie, and shoes. Jaya covered herself with a few sarees and wore my socks on her hands and feet. We managed to get through the coldest night either of us had ever experienced.

Things warmed up the next morning. We returned to Srinagar and spent the night in a small hotel. The next day, we took a bus to Pathankot and a night train to Delhi. And yes, we shopped for cherries in Srinagar and packed them in a tin box!

CHAPTER TWENTY-ONE

As the train pulled into New Delhi station, we were a bit scared. We had heard a lot about *'Dilli ka Thug'* (crooks of Delhi). We were to stay at the Gujarati Samaj Guest House, meant primarily for Gujarati's visiting Delhi from India and all over the world. They provided accommodation and food from their in-house restaurant at the most economical rates.

We stood in a corner wondering how to get there. Take a taxi? Or an auto-rickshaw? Since this was my maiden visit to Delhi, I had no clue how to navigate the city. We even considered public transport – the local buses, but how would we haul our luggage?

Just as we were about to step out of the station, we noticed a young man, maybe in his early 20s, walk toward us. "You want to go to Gujarati Samaj?" he asked in authentic Gujarati. What a relief! I nodded. "Come along," he said. He helped us carry our luggage to his auto rickshaw. Before we started our journey, he showed us the auto fare indicator – meter. It was a small round metal container with figures. He asked us to verify that the meter was starting with its reading at zero. I told him, "No, it's ok. How far is Gujarati Samaj? No need to show us the reading, we trust you." He smiled, which we took to be a thank you gesture. After 30 minutes, we reached Gujarati Samaj. The meter reading was six rupees and fifty paise. I thanked him two or three times.

Fortunately for us, rooms were still available. We checked in, took a short nap, showered, and were ready to head out. Our priority was to return to the Delhi railway booking centre and reconfirm our seats for our onward journey to Bombay, particularly since it was a break journey on a stopover ticket. While our booking was done, we had to reconfirm it at least 72 hours before departure.

We hired an auto-rickshaw, this time without any luggage. We looked very much like locals. We asked the driver to take us to the first-class railway booking office near Plaza Cinema. Expecting another thirty-minute ride, we were surprised when we reached in just a few minutes with the total fare of one rupee and twenty-five paise!

It was clear that the driver who we used when we first arrived had taken us for a joyride.

Yet, we did not harbour any ill-will towards him. He charged us a bit more, but in the bargain he showed us some parts of Delhi like Darya Ganj, acted as a guide, and above all, made us comfortable, bringing us safely to our destination.

We were to stay in Delhi for three days. The temperature was around 44-45 degrees Celsius throughout, a 40-year high. To make matters worse, our room did not have a cooler. And cold drinking water was also not available. The next day, early in the evening, before heading out for sightseeing, we sprinkled water on the tiled floor of our room, hoping it would cool things down. This time, instead of taking an auto-rickshaw, we walked towards Kashmiri Gate, where we had seen some hand pump vendors selling cold water. We took our thermos bottle along. After walking for about 30 minutes, we reached Kashmiri Gate. We filled our water bottle for 25 paise.

It was 7:30 p.m. by the time we finished our dinner at a street food joint. It was getting dark. The street lights were not adequate. Rather than walk in the dark in an unknown city, we decided to head back to the Samaj on a local bus. While we knew that it was a straight road, we were not aware of the specific name of the bus stop we had to get off at. The name of the street where Gujarati Samaj was located was Ludlow Castle Road (Raj Bhavan Path). We waited for a while at the bus stop. We boarded the next bus that stopped. There were hardly any passengers on the bus. Our conversation with the conductor was interesting.

"Ticket?" he asked.

"Gujarati Samaj," I said.

"This bus doesn't go there," he firmly responded.

"Conductor, it is about two or three stops from where we got into the bus – Kashmiri Gate," I said, somewhat confused.

"That will not do. You have to name the bus stop," he insisted.

Still confused, I said, "I do not know the name of the stop."

He responded, "If you do not know, how will I give you a ticket? And unless I give you a ticket you will not be allowed to alight."

"Okay. Give me a ticket for the last stop of your bus," I said thinking that would solve the problem.

He immediately said, "No, I don't want to overcharge you. Besides, by the way, this is a ring service and it goes round and round until it goes to the garage."

Jaya and I looked at each other, confused. I thought our confusion was apparent on our faces.

He smiled, "Get down at the next bus stop and turn left at the first street."

I asked him, "How much for the ticket?"

"Nothing. I was just pulling your leg," he said in a friendly tone.

The conductor was in his mid-40s and we were in our early 20s.

"Thank you, sir!" I said with some relief.

"Go carefully," he warned.

I still cannot forget his friendly smile.

On the day we were checking out, we found that the cherries packed in the tin box had breathed their last due to the extreme weather differences between Kashmir and Delhi.

By now, I had just Rs. 38 in my wallet. We decided to preserve Rs. 20 for some emergency or just in case no one came to pick us up from the station if they had not received our postcard. With a balance of Rs.18, we had to manage tea, lunch, and dinner. We estimated that it was possible and we could still save about Rs. 5 for extra expenses if any.

As our train left Delhi station, I remembered that my B.A. final exam results were to be released the next day. In those days, exam results were printed in the local newspapers. So when our train reached Dahanu Station the next morning, the first thing I did was to buy the newspaper.

I dug out my exam slip with my candidate number. Anxiously, I browsed through the thousands of numbers printed on the page and quickly found my number. I was successful. I was a graduate! I had cleared my B. A (Hons) exam.

We finally reached Mumbai. At the station, we were greeted by two of my brothers-in-law. We reached home, the 20 rupees note still intact.

I now prepared myself for new commitments and new responsibilities.

CHAPTER TWENTY-TWO

Life was moving at its own pace, with its share of ups and downs. It was swinging between good and bad times. Both successes and failures have their share in everyone's life. Overall, I had no major complaints about life.

One evening, when I returned from the office feeling more tired than usual, I heard a lady guest in our house saying, "Nowadays, daughters-in-law do not listen to us, but what can we say when even our maidservants do not listen to us."

I lost my temper and shouted at her, "How dare you compare daughters-in-law with maidservants? Please leave our house at once."

She said, "I came here because of your parents. Who are you to ask me to get out? If I go now, I will never come to this house again."

Raising my voice further, I said, "You are free to do what you want to do but leave my house right now." I noticed that my mother and father did not intervene and did not say anything. She started crying and left.

After she left, my parents were upset with my attitude and my outburst. My father said, "We all know her nature. It was not good on your part to behave like this with an older person."

I was also very angry and upset but did not say a word. I simply walked away. I did not speak to anyone that night, except Jaya who tried to pacify me.

I had calmed down by the next morning. I realized that my reaction was extreme. It was insulting. I felt bad too. At that time, I decided I would never allow anyone to interfere in our home. And I would never interfere in anyone's house. This has remained my principle even today.

As time passed by, the lady once again began visiting us, but stopped gossiping about or interfering in our house. After my father passed away, as long as she was alive, she would tie a *Rakhi* to me. If she was unable to come to our house, I would go to her house for *Rakhi*. I don't think she ever held a grudge against us. Without regard for the past incident, she loved Jaya and me, always showering her blessings upon us from the bottom of her heart. In particular, because of Jaya's sober nature, she had a special feeling and soft corner for her. In her old age, Jaya visited her and kept her company. She liked that. She always said that Jaya was her favourite daughter-in-law.

"Choru Kachoru thai, pan mavtar kamavtar na thai." Children may forget their duties towards parents, but parents never forget their duties towards their children.

CHAPTER TWENTY-THREE

Two years after our wedding, Jaya was expecting our first child. We were thrilled at the thought of becoming parents. I had started counting the days. In the meantime, *Adha* who lived in Abu Dhabi invited me to visit UAE. He, along with my parents was looking forward to me finding a job in the UAE and settling there. As I mentioned earlier, I could not disagree with the views of my elders/parents. I was not at all comfortable with the thought that when our first baby arrived, I would not be with Jaya. She tried to convince me to stay back in Abu Dhabi if I got a good offer. I told her I would see but was not prepared at all for such a scenario.

With these thoughts in mind, I reluctantly agreed to visit the UAE. It was my first ever experience taking a flight and also the first time I was visiting a foreign country. I was not excited about my first flight abroad and was more interested in planning my return date. As we neared our destination – Abu Dhabi, I felt a sense of joy as I would meet my brother and sister-in-law. Since my brother had already arranged for a visitor's visa, it was a smooth exit from immigration. He had come to pick me up at the airport. While driving home, I saw desert all over, but with wide and well-paved roads, a few tall buildings, and lots of ongoing construction activity – infrastructure for growth. This indicated future planning.

I wanted to resist the temptation of getting carried away by all this. However, it was a struggle to not fall in love with the city. As we got closer to his home, I decided to change the direction of my thoughts. We reached his building, parked the car, and stepped into the elevator.

After lunch and an afternoon siesta, my brother showed me the developing city of Abu Dhabi. While driving around, I could visualize the future of the city. It was such a tempting environment that I could not help but praise it lavishly. My brother asked me how I liked the city and whether I would like to settle there. I said, "The city is good but I want to go back to Bombay in two or three weeks, as my priority is to welcome my first child."

He tried to convince me, but I remained firm. He said, "Okay, take a week to think before you make a final decision. As such, with already eight years of banking experience, you should easily be able to get a job here. As the city is developing fast there will be many opportunities for you." Almost every day, he arranged a meeting with one bank manager or another. After learning about my experience, without exception, they invited me to join them.

A week to ten days later, my brother tried to explain to me how bright my future would be in the UAE. Our lifestyle would improve, our financial position would strengthen, we would have all the luxuries we dreamed of, and so on.

As tempting as it was, for the reasons I mentioned earlier, I did not want to confirm that I indeed wanted to shape my future in Abu Dhabi. On the contrary, I went to the travel agent's office to book my return ticket to Bombay. The executive attending to me was surprised I was going back in only 23 days. She said, "Are you not getting a job? If you are interested I will speak to my boss just now and you will get a job easily."

I smiled and said, "Thank you. I have had many offers since I came to Abu Dhabi but have to go back for personal reasons." She was perplexed but we did not discuss it further.

One thing I had observed while in Abu Dhabi was that domestic help was not easily available. No maids. No cooks. I saw my sister-in-law slogging the whole day to manage the house. Despite being extremely busy every day, my brother and sister-in-law always encouraged me to stay back in Abu Dhabi. Every evening we used to go out for a drive and weekends on outings. When I turn the pages of my memory book, I distinctly remember that they were disappointed in my decision not to settle in Abu Dhabi. But again, my priority at that time was my first child.

I must admit that when boarding the plane for the return journey home, I thought that maybe sometime in the future I would go back. After all, opportunities extend their hand several times in life. You need to grab only those which you can handle.

CHAPTER TWENTY-FOUR

In a space of three years, we were blessed with two children. First a daughter and then a son. By now, my father had retired from the bank. It was now time for me to apply for my promotion which I had delayed seeking despite being eligible, following through on my resolution to do so only after my father had retired, thus avoiding accusations of favouritism.

Just five days before my promotion interview, my father's friend from the neighbouring building returned from Nathdwara, a temple town, famous for its Krishna temple which housed the deity of Shrinathji, a 14th-century, seven-year-old infant incarnation of Krishna.

He paid us an urgent visit to let us know that my father had suffered a heart attack. My parents had a circular train ticket for their pilgrimage tour and Nathdwara was the last destination where they were to stay for a month or so. As there was no direct dialling facility then, being concerned and not being able to ascertain what his condition was, I decided to travel that very night. Jaya, my daughter Rachana, younger sister Pramila, my nephew Prakash and I managed to get train tickets for the night train to Ahmedabad, from where we took a bus in the morning to Nathdwara. Rachit, my son, was not yet born.

We reached Nathdwara in the evening. My father was in bed looking exhausted. He gestured to welcome us. My mother explained what had happened. I immediately went to meet the attending doctor, actually the only doctor in Nathdwara. He did not mince his words when giving me my father's health status. According to him, my father was not in his comfort zone. Medical facilities were limited in a small town such as Nathdwara so had to move him to Udaipur, a larger city about 60 km away. Unfortunately, no physical movements were permitted and we would be able to transfer him to Udaipur only after three or four days. Taking him to Bombay was risky and out of the question.

I was very nervous as I had never encountered a responsibility or situation of this magnitude before this. I returned home, had dinner, and went to sleep. Jaya, in a reassuring tone, said, "Let us see his condition tomorrow, then we will decide."

During a typical day, there are multiple *darshans* or prayers that devotees can avail of at the Nathdwara temple.

The first *darshan* of Shreeji Bava, as our deity is affectionately called, was at 5:30 a.m. the next morning. Jaya and I woke up early for this *darshan* called *Mangala*. After the *Mangala Aarti*, I stood quietly in a corner and closed my eyes to pray. For a minute or two, I prayed with full concentration. Forgetting about everything else, myself, my surroundings, I begged, "O Shreeji Bava, until today, I have not asked for anything from you, but today I am asking you – if knowingly I have not harmed anybody or even thought about it, then when I go home from here, my father must tell me, 'Let us go for sightseeing to Udaipur'. If this happens, only then will I believe in you and your existence. Else, I will never come to Nathdwara again to do your *darshan*."

I have never been able to achieve the concentration of those one or two minutes ever again in my life. After *darshan*, as we were sipping morning tea, I told Jaya about my stupidity. Staying as calm as ever, she said, "The thought of you specifically asking Shreeji Bava was inappropriate. He would understand your state of mind on His own. One should never throw a challenge to God."

We went home. My father was still in bed with no visible improvement in his health. With only three days left for my interview, I reconciled myself to be mentally prepared for missing out on the promotion opportunity. Perhaps that was to be my destiny. After about 15 minutes or so, my father asked me to come closer. In a low voice, he asked me to help him get up. I made him sit up, with a pillow to support his back. After about another 15 minutes, he said, "Vijay, I am feeling slightly better. Can you take me to the bathroom?" I declined, saying the doctor had strictly advised complete bed rest for him. He said, "Let me try." His voice was still low and he seemed tired, but I lent him support to get up. He was able to walk slowly to the bathroom, come back and sit on the bed. He asked for tea. Then all of a sudden, he said, "I am feeling much better." After about five minutes he added, "I think I am now feeling confident. Let us go to Udaipur and we will come back in the evening."

I became emotional. I had tears in my eyes. I ran down to do the next *darshan*, *Shringar*. I did *Sashtang Dandavat* to Shreeji Bava, lying face down on the floor with my hands outstretched and folded, an act of complete submission to the deity. This proved that any prayer performed with a pure heart will never go in vain. I repeat, I have never achieved such concentration while doing *darshan* and prayer again. Maybe Shreeji Bava did not want me to become greedy and a habitual beggar. I became a strong believer that whatever God does for us, is for our betterment.

Against medical advice, we went to Udaipur in a taxi. I had full faith in Shreeji Bava. We had an enjoyable outing for the entire day. I was a bit tense for the first half, but in the latter I was confident there would be no complications.

We returned, before dinner. I saw that my father was his usual self. We could not believe that in the morning he was bedridden. I informed him about my interview in three days. He looked at me with a non-approving face of my decision to come to Nathdwara with such an important milestone right ahead. Immediately, he said, "Let us all go back to Bombay tomorrow." We exchanged views and deliberated on the situation. In the end, it was decided that I would take the night bus to Ahmedabad and the morning train from there to Bombay so I could reach Bombay by night. I could then appear for my interview the next day.

Shreeji Bava ensured that our plan went through smoothly including me getting a train reservation at the last minute. I appeared for the interview. It went well. I was confident of the outcome. I was not disappointed. I was just glad to be successful and my name was on top of the list. It had to be so, as my candidate serial number was 'Bom-1'. It was an emotional moment. It is rightly said – emotions are extended thought processes.

CHAPTER TWENTY-FIVE

I got the promotion. I was now an officer placed in the Audit Department. Generally, whosoever got a posting in this department was very happy. Because this department completed audits for all branches in the country, one had the opportunity to do 'Bharat Darshan' (travel all over India) at the bank's cost. The bank paid an allowance that was good enough to take care of all outstation expenses and more often than not, one even saved a good amount in the end. The base salary was saved. The audit posting was for a minimum of five years. Additionally, with having to eat food cooked in restaurants, you were rewarded with acidity, ulcers, and other gastro issues.

Frankly, I was not happy with my audit job. I would have to remain away from home and family for at least 200 days or so in a year. Food would also be a challenge since I did not eat onion and garlic (still do not). It was never a religious matter for me, but I had not acquired a taste for it since childhood. I had also heard a lot about discrimination between juniors and seniors. Seniors would often humiliate juniors, ordering them to run errands for them, forcing them to perform personal chores. Juniors were expected to 'respect' seniors by allowing them to enter the bus first and not occupy a window seat without their permission. If asked to buy fruits, juniors would have to buy them and be reimbursed only, if in their opinion, the price paid was fair and the fruits were good for consumption. One couldn't object, let alone raise their voice against this injustice. Those who did so faced consequences, bordering on mental torture.

This is not an exaggeration. With all this frightening feedback, I was not comfortable going for outstation audits.

However, I managed to remain in the local audit unit for a considerable amount of time. Then the inevitable happened, and I was told to prepare to go out of Bombay for an audit. Fortunately, the city was Ahmedabad, in the neighbouring state of Gujarat. While not thrilled, I was relieved that at least food without onion and garlic would be easily available. I have no hesitation in admitting that the Head of the Department of Audit was my father's colleague and a good friend.

There were a total of 23 officers in the city who were assigned to complete an audit in the Ahmedabad main branch. Remember, we had no computers in those days, so it took an army of people to complete an audit. The team leader was an elderly gentleman Mr Bipin Palekar, who was to retire from the bank in another six months. His two deputies were Mr Kulkarni and Mr Sanghvi. Mr Kulkarni was known for his arrogance and dictating nature. He was highly unpopular with the juniors.

Mr Sanghvi, on the other hand, was a first-time deputy, so his track record in that capacity was not known.

We left for the audit by train, reaching Ahmedabad early in the morning. After checking into the hotel and freshening up, we took auto-rickshaws to reach the Ahmedabad main branch.

The first day of the audit felt very much like a raid by investigating agencies, with several people suddenly descending on branches, that were never be informed in advance.

We were instructed not to get friendly with the staff and not to answer sensitive questions without referring to the team leader or his deputies. Our first job was to check cash and cash related transactions such as stamp papers. The main branch also served as a currency chest. The primary role of the currency chest was cash management – to distribute notes and coins received from the mint through the Reserve Bank of India (RBI), India's Central Bank, to other bank branches throughout the region.

I had not encountered any 'dictatorship' during my local audit and was high on self-confidence. To count the notes, Mr Kulkarni distributed the cash bundles to us. The team leader's role was only to oversee the counting. Once we finished counting a bundle, and if found to be accurate, we had to initial the first note to indicate that it was complete. Once we finished the packet, we had to initial it.

I did my job diligently. When I finished counting one bundle, Mr Kulkarni handed me a bundle that had been half counted and asked me to count the balance notes. This was not the right process from any angle. However, I did not say a word and did what he asked. After counting, I told him the number of notes counted by me. He said "Correct". This was his casual attitude with everyone, and that bothered me.

At around 12:30 p.m. ten officers took a lunch break. For nine of us, it was our first official visit to Ahmedabad, but one officer was on his second trip. Thankfully, he knew of a vegetarian restaurant that was good and reasonably priced.

We placed our orders. The food was good. The bill was about Rs. 180. As was my habit, I picked up the tab. I was the junior-most and so it seemed to make sense. When we exited the restaurant, everyone asked what they owed. I told them it would be Rs. 18 per head. "I did not have buttermilk," one officer said. Another commented he has eaten one less dish. When the third officer was about to speak, I stopped him and said, "Don't worry, today's lunch is on me." They pretended to say that it was not correct and that I must take their contribution. However, with just a little insistence, they said, "OK, thank you."

I decided to raise this issue in the evening team meeting.

We returned to the branch and resumed the note counting process. I got a packet with new Rs. 20 bundles. It still had the RBI label on it with the date on which it was technically released. I took a close look at the packet as it was my first experience handling a newly sealed packet of currency notes. I carefully opened the packet. I took out one bundle and began counting. The signature of the RBI Governor attracted my attention. I finished counting the bundle. I picked up another bundle and was shocked by what I saw. This bundle had the signature of an RBI Governor who had been appointed much after the date on the packet, maybe even two years after. I was alarmed. I took a close look and again read the date on the packet. There was no doubt. This bundle had a signature of a Governor who was appointed much after the release of these notes. I also found many differences in the RBI logo (tree/tiger). When I further compared it with other denomination notes, I found as many as five to six differences. I was aghast!

I went to the chief cashier of the branch who was overseeing our note counting operation. I said, "Sir, can I keep the packet cover with me as a memento?" He was fine with it as the cover would anyway be trashed. I thanked him and put it in my trouser pocket. For a moment, I thought of bringing this up to my seniors, but because this would be a sensitive subject for the local branch officials, I decided to instead discuss it in the evening team meeting.

Before leaving for the day, I went to the chief cashier to thank him again. I also asked him, "The date on the currency note packet – is that the date on which the packet is released by RBI or is it the date on which the packet is received by the bank?" He responded that the date on the packet was indeed the date on which RBI released it and sent such packets to various banks. That confirmed my doubt that something was not right.

We were told to assemble at 9 p.m. in the team leader's hotel room for the evening meeting. I raised my hand as the meeting was about to begin. I was permitted to speak.

I started with the lunch expenses experience, suggesting that the bill be split equally among all the officers who go for lunch in a group. One of the officers who was a part of our lunch group said that it was common practice during outstation audits that the junior-most officer in the group took care of such things. He complained that he also did the same thing when he was a junior officer. I was surprised. I looked at Mr Palekar, our team leader for an answer. Before he could speak, his deputy Mr Kulkarni jumped in, "That is correct. Since you were the junior most in that group it was your duty to keep a watch on such things."

I protested, "Sorry, I cannot follow such a practice. I am on the official duty of the bank, not of other individuals." Everyone appeared to be stunned. There was pin-drop silence. It was as if I was the first junior officer who spoke so bluntly about this issue. I added, "In that case, starting tomorrow, I will go to lunch and dinner on my own. If anyone wants to join me, they are welcome." No one spoke a word.

As Mr Kulkarni was about to speak, I said, "There is one more topic I want to draw everyone's attention to. This might be a serious issue." I briefed them on what I had observed earlier that morning. I showed them the packet cover, the bundle label. I also informed them that I had brought these with the permission of the chief cashier. Next, I started to explain the differences in the RBI logo appearing on it compared with other denomination notes. In support, I pulled out some old Rs. 20 notes from my packet.

Mr Kulkarni interrupted me saying that what I was sharing was not our lookout. Our job was simply to count the notes.

I asked, "Sir, what if such notes are counterfeit currency?"

He responded, "You will not be responsible for that."

I retorted, "If something like this comes to our attention, are we still supposed to continue counting and report a correct cash balance? What if genuine notes are replaced with counterfeit ones?"

Nobody had an answer.

Mr Palekar also looked around the room. All he could do was just shrug his shoulders. He asked to meet me alone after the meeting. Once again I explained everything to him and shared my apprehensions by showing him the proof that I had brought from the branch. He agreed with me, "I do not know what we should do next. This is the first time I have come across such a situation." I told him, "Sir, the day after tomorrow, on Saturday, I will be going to Bombay as my mother is leaving for Abu Dhabi on Sunday. If you permit me a day's leave on Monday, I will go to our bank's central chief cashier Mr Gandhi and ask for his opinion and get a clarification on this matter." He nodded his approval but requested me not to involve him in this situation as he had only a few months to go before his retirement. He also asked me to not let Mr Gandhi know that he was aware of this matter or that it was discussed in the team meeting. I assured him, "Sir, thank you very much. I will take care of that."

I travelled to Bombay. On Monday, I went to meet Mr Gandhi and apprised him of my findings and apprehensions. He was a senior official of the bank who had spent all his banking years in the cash department. When I showed him the proof – the cover, label etc., he asked me to wait outside and called his two assistants.

After about half an hour, he came out and said, "Son, let us go and meet the Chairman. He was excited but also worried."

He asked me to wait outside the Chairman's cabin and went inside. I was excited and preparing to present myself before the Chairman, anticipating appreciation.

After what seemed an eternity, Mr Gandhi came out looking dejected and disappointed. I wondered what might have happened. He told me, "Go inside, the Chairman wants to talk to you."

I went in. The Chairman looked at me and signalled me to take a seat. He said, "Can you show me the cover and other proofs which you have brought from Ahmedabad Branch?" I showed him. He snatched it from my hands.

"Any more proof?" he asked tersely.

"No Sir," I responded.

"Good," he said.

He then tore the material I had handed him into small pieces and threw it into the trash basket. He stared at me, extended his hand to shake and said, "If you have any work in the future, come to me. You can go now."

I came out. Mr Gandhi simply asked me to walk back to his cabin with him. Neither of us spoke a word. I had a thousand questions running through my mind. He ordered tea and asked, "What happened?" I shared with him exactly what had transpired in the Chairman's chamber and then asked him, "Sir, he made you sit in his cabin for almost an hour. What did you both discuss? If you trust me, please tell me, I am eager to know."

"Son, I know your father very well. I have learned a lot from him including what is sincerity and honesty. He is sincerity and honesty personified. Now listen carefully. I gave all the details to the Chairman. He called someone from the Finance Ministry and wanted to talk to the Finance Secretary who took 15 to 20 minutes to return the call. The Chairman briefed him about the whole issue. I do not know what the Secretary said, but they disconnected the phone. A few minutes later, the Secretary called back. This time, the Chairman simply responded 'Yes, Sir; yes Sir, yes, Sir' and at the end said, 'I will take care of it.' He cut the call and said, "Mr Gandhi, send that boy in and yes, remember we have to close this chapter here and now. I came out and sent you in. Son, I feel your efforts to dig out the truth has been in vain. Anyway, get back to your work. Don't discuss these details with anyone. God bless you."

I came back to Ahmedabad to resume my duty. Mr Palekar asked for an update. I simply told him that the Chairman said he would look into the matter. I never experimented with the concept of trust.

CHAPTER TWENTY-SIX

The next day, I was given an assignment to audit the Fixed Deposit (FD) section. I was happy because I had spent about ten years in this section of the bank. Bank FDs were considered to be one of the main avenues for investment other than the stock market, which was considered a 'Satta Bazaar' (Speculative Market).

Everything was manual in those days. Calculators, which had been introduced only a year ago, were still a bit of a luxury. With my overall knowledge of the FD section, I presumed that regional branches would not have as much volume as the main branch. I was correct. Before I proceed, let me share with you that interest calculation on fixed deposits was done with the help of a 'Ready Reckoner'. For example, to calculate interest on Rs. 35,555 at a certain interest rate, we first had to calculate the interest on Rs. 30,000 for the number of days the FD is parked. Then for Rs. 5000, Rs. 500 Rs. 50 Rs. 5 respectively. These figures had to be jotted down. Then we would manually add up to the total interest on Rs. 35,555 for one fixed deposit. This process had to be repeated for all the others.

Even balancing ledgers and registers was done manually. I was confident that, with my experience in the main branch, my audit in this section would be smooth and fast.

I started to audit and found several errors including incorrect interest calculations and irregularities in opening fixed deposit accounts. I discussed these with the Sectional Head Mr Sonpal and requested him to get the errors corrected within three days.

While checking whether balancing with central ledgers was done regularly, I was shocked to find that the department balancing had not done for the past nine months. It was clear that nobody had even made any attempt to balance the books. This was a serious lapse with a provision for stricter steps and immediate notification to the head office. The head office would then send a special team from Bombay to scrutinize every single entry in all related documents. This was to evaluate and rule out fraud.

Instead of immediately reporting this matter, I thought it would be better to first discuss with Mr Sonpal and ask him to clarify. He was nervous when I brought it up with him.

He said, "Sir, the responsibility for this job is with two staff members but both of them are staff union leaders. They don't listen to me. But please give me three-four days and I will try to finish the work."

I told him, "*Saheb* (Sir), first, please do not call me sir. You are much older than me and a senior officer. I am a junior officer and much younger than you. I am embarrassed when you call me 'Sir'."

In an emotional tone, he said, "You are the first audit officer to say so. All other audit officers treat us as if we are their slaves and they are our masters."

I responded, "Sir, today I'm an audit officer, tomorrow I may not be. I do not believe that audit officers are superior."

I returned to my desk, the conversation with Mr Sonpal still playing on my mind. At the end of the day when everyone had left and Mr Sonpal was alone, I approached him and said, "Sir, if you permit, can we work together to regularize the books?" He was touched and tears filled his eyes. He asked, "Would you do clerical work?" I told him, "Sir, when you as a senior officer are willing to do clerical work, why wouldn't I? It would be my pleasure to assist you."

We started regularizing the books. It took us two hours to finish the work which had been pending for the past nine months. He was amazed at my total involvement. He was speechless. Then he invited me for lunch at his house the next Sunday. I agreed.

The next day, Mr Sonpal described to his staff who were responsible for the pending work, how I had finished the work with him. They did not like that. They came to me and said, "You are an audit officer. How can you do clerical work?" I told them, "Brothers, we all are members of one bank family, aren't we? How would it make a difference if I do the work or you do the work? After all, it is work of the bank, right?" After that, I received full cooperation from both those staff members for the rest of my time in Ahmedabad. We became friendly, but just short of being friends.

On Sunday, I went to Mr Sonpal's house for lunch. Every member of his family was present. At lunch, he told me, "Vijaybhai, I don't think I will come across another audit officer like you." I responded, "Sir, can I share a secret with you? I had a personal interest in this. To that extent I was selfish." He wondered what my self-interest could be. I said, "When I have done the work myself, there was no chance of doubting my work especially whenever the books were balanced, right?" He broke out into a loud laugh.

Whenever I was placed in a situation where I needed to change my approach to any issue from what I had originally envisioned, I did it. Maybe I have been gifted not to miss the essence of the situation.

CHAPTER TWENTY-SEVEN

We met on the first Friday of the audit assignment for payers of respective bills to receive reimbursement of their weekly expenses. All the bills were to be checked by Mr Kulkarni. After review, he would send these to be signed off by the team leader and then to the head office for processing. Within a day, our respective accounts would be credited. No questions were asked as long as the deputy team leader and the team leader approved it.

I was surprised to find that even scrutiny of bills was done based on seniority. Mine were the last ones to be scrutinized, as I was the junior-most audit officer on the team. Mr Kulkarni glanced at the items which I claimed for reimbursement. With a surprised look, he asked me, "Vijay, where are *coolie* (porterage) charges, weekly auto rickshaw fare to and from the hotel and bank, and your laundry bill?"

I was puzzled, "Sir, I did not hire any porter at Ahmedabad Station. I have been walking from the hotel to the bank and back, except on the first day. I have been washing my clothes and not given any for laundry. How can I bill for such items when I have not spent anything on them?"

I could tell by looking around the room, that the atmosphere had become tense.

Mr Kulkarni seemed irritated and declared, "All these expenses are allowable for reimbursement. Twenty-two of us have claimed bills for these items and if you do not do so, then there will be a question mark against our claims."

I responded, "I am not questioning your claims. I firmly believe that we must find irregularities by any bank staff including any false claims for medical expenses or leave fare concessions. I am very sorry, you all can go ahead but my conscience will not permit me to join you. No, I can't do that."

Not a single officer spoke a word including Mr Kulkarni. Mr Palekar took me aside and told me to just follow others. "This is my last tour and I am going to retire shortly after this. I will be under tremendous pressure. I request you to agree."

I noticed he was just short of pleading with folded hands. I looked at him and nodded. I turned to face others and said, "Okay, I agree to raise the bill for these items as others have claimed, but with one condition. I will set aside whatever amount I get reimbursed that I have not originally spent. At the end of the tour, I will throw a party with that amount. All of us will attend that party. Can you agree with me on that?"

Everybody clapped. I heard a chorus of 'yes, yes' in the room. However, I was sad from within.

I had come across a bunch of hypocrites across different age groups and different segments of society. They were a club of hypocrites. No form is to be filled for membership in this club. If one is a hypocrite, by default he becomes a member of that club. Hypocrisy cannot be concealed – it has a habit of self-proclamation.

CHAPTER TWENTY-EIGHT

After ten days, at the evening team meeting, I announced that I had completed the audit of the fixed deposit section. I shared my report and asked to be given other work.

Mr Kulkarni interrupted me. "Impossible Vijay. The last time it took me two months to complete the same audit. I am sure you have not done it properly."

Everyone was shocked that the second senior-most officer on the team took 60 days to complete what I had done in ten days.

I responded, "Anyone is free to cross-check or verify if I have completed everything required to be done. I have put my initials as a confirmation of my checking. Make no mistake, I have not just checked randomly, but completed a thorough check."

Mr Kulkarni immediately asked one of my seniors to cross-check my work the next day at random to verify my claim that I had completed my job diligently. For an immediate moment, I felt a little slighted, but was happy because once the random check was done, a question inevitably would arise, "What was Mr Kulkarni doing for 60 days?" I was confident.

Mr Sanghvi, who was going to cross-check my work, told me the next morning before he began his verification, "I have a good friend in your section who always speaks highly about you. I am sure you have done your work properly, but I have no option." I said, "Mr Sanghvi, thank you for your confidence in me. It is all right. You do your job and let me know if I have missed out on some major or even minor things." And then I asked him, "Who are you going to submit your report to – Mr Kulkarni or Mr Palekar?" He said, "Mr Palekar, of course."

He spent a full day cross verifying important items. When he heard from Mr Sonpal how I had helped them get the pending balancing done, Mr Sanghvi was also moved. He appreciated this by saying, "I have been in audit for ten years. You are the first officer who has done this. I am going to mention this in my report." I told him, "Sir, I thought that if I did the job, I would be one hundred per cent satisfied that everything was okay. Whenever errors were found in the process, Mr Sonpal corrected them then and there."

When Mr Sanghvi's report was read by Mr Palekar in the team meeting, Mr Kulkarni walked out. I subsequently started hearing that the attitudes of seniors towards juniors were changing all over India, as word had spread of what had transpired. I felt satisfied and happy. Had I been a catalyst for change? It was immensely satisfying when some of the junior officers of my batch who were on duty elsewhere called to congratulate me saying how the working environment had changed for them too.

CHAPTER TWENTY-NINE

While on duty in Ahmedabad, I developed acute uneasiness one evening. I requested one of my colleagues to come to my room. I kept the door open to avoid getting up. The next morning, when I opened my eyes, I was told by my colleague that I had become unconscious. They had to summon a doctor who gave me some emergency treatment.

I had woken up relatively fresh but still felt tired. I pulled on for a few days, but everyone was sympathetic and caring seeing how pale I had become. I simply could not gather myself. I was just not myself.

This was my first health scare. Suddenly and surprisingly, I felt I was losing my confidence. I talked to Mr Palekar about my health concerns and asked if he would permit me to return to Bombay early. He asked for a day or two to talk to his boss. They both agreed to shorten my audit trip. I thanked Mr Palekar and let him know that I would go back as soon as I completed my assignment on hand, maybe after four or five days. He asked me whether I wanted to return earlier, even the next day, and expressed his willingness to depute someone from the team to complete the rest of my assignment.

I again thanked him but insisted that I be allowed to complete my assignment, which I did within a week.

It was now time to say 'thank you' to all my team members for their support when I needed it the most. Before departing, as promised, I threw a party, the expenses of which were met by the money I got from my reimbursement. Everyone attended.

I returned to Bombay. We were now blessed with a son. First a daughter and now a son. In banking terms, I would say that the ledger of life was balanced.

CHAPTER THIRTY

Sadly, I was not able to rejoice in the birth of my son. For some reason, at the stroke of five each evening, I would go numb and start slipping into sleep mode, not wanting to talk to anyone. It was strange that the next morning I would be fresh again as if nothing had happened the previous day. But come 5 p.m., again the same numbness, the same sleepiness. This went on for a couple of months.

I was also fed up. Slipping into depression right at the stroke of five was puzzling for everyone. My mother and Jaya took me to all possible temples, astrologers, and performed many *pujas*. Nothing was working. My health concerns started to bother me more and more. I consulted a neurologist and underwent various medical investigations like EEG and so on. All the doctors said this condition was psychological. But what type of psychological condition was this? No doctor could diagnose it or be specific.

Gradually, I began developing suicidal thoughts. During one such gloomy evening, Jaya and I went for a walk with our one-month-old son. I was carrying him and he almost slipped out of my hands as I was not awake. Jaya caught him before he fell. Even today, I shudder to think of that moment. It was terrible. That night I cried like a baby.

Jaya would always ask me to seek the blessings of Mataji, who she considered her godmother. Jaya believed She had divine powers and believed that She would heal me and pull us out of trouble. I never agreed. I was dismissive and critical. I refused to believe that any normal human being could have such superpowers.

With my condition worsening, Jaya pleaded with me, "What is the harm in visiting Mataji? Let us please try." Under the shadow of developing suicidal thoughts, I relented and agreed. We went to Her house. I had never met Her before. I bowed to Her. She firmly patted my back, gave her blessings and a fist of uncooked rice as *Prasad* to consume in a few portions. She asked us to return for another blessing after two days. We did so. She did not do anything additional this time – just blessings and rice to consume.

After three visits to her, on the fourth day, I was all right and back to my normal self even after 5 p.m.

I leave it to all of you to conclude what that could be – a miracle or something else? I do not have an answer. But I realized that when you are going through a bad or lean phase, explore every unexplored remedy. Do not make it an excuse to punish yourself until then.

CHAPTER THIRTY-ONE

My next audit assignment was to Dhulia, a small city in the western part of Maharashtra. The duration of this assignment was likely to be about two months. By this time, I was fed up and did not want to go out of Bombay on office duty for a longer duration. It was almost 10 months since my promotion. The probation period was 11 months, which meant I had only 30 days to decide whether to continue as an audit officer, obey orders for outstation duty or resign.

I had an option to opt for reversion to clerical cadre. I applied for transfer out of the audit section on medical grounds and if not possible, for reversion to clerical cadre. There was no response for 15 days. With only 15 days left, I was beginning to get anxious. My father advised me to give priority to my health.

As time kept ticking, I remembered that when I met the Chairman while I was on duty at Ahmedabad he had said that I could see him at any time if it concerned work-related issues. I was not sure whether he would agree to meet me, let alone remember me. I waited for one more week. With only three days left and with no response from the Personnel Department (HR), I decided to attempt to meet the Chairman.

I went to his office. His assistant asked me whether I had an appointment and why I wanted to meet him. I responded that while I did not have an appointment, it was important for me to meet him to discuss an urgent matter.

She hesitated, expressing her inability to allow me to see him. I pleaded and requested that she inform the Chairman that I was Vijay Thariani, Audit Officer, who had come to see him with the Chief Cashier Mr Gandhi, a few weeks ago. Seemingly unhappy with my insistence, she reluctantly talked to the Chairman through the intercom. She asked me to return in an hour.

I thought it would be a good idea to brief Mr Gandhi about why I wanted to meet the Chairman. He asked me to go ahead warning me to not be optimistic considering the Chairman's response to the Ahmedabad episode. "You could have tried meeting him before you submitted the letter of reversion/transfer. Anyway good luck."

I was a bit shaken but consoled myself that I was not going to lose my job. The worst case was that my transfer application would be declined and I would become a clerk again. I was mentally prepared. This thought gave me some comfort and enabled me to prepare to talk to the Chairman and try to seek a favour if possible.

After an hour, I went to the Chairman's office again and surprisingly found his assistant to be extremely courteous. She politely asked me to wait for a few minutes. After five minutes or so, she directed me to accompany her, guided me to the Chairman's chamber, opened the door and let me in.

Just as I was entering, I could feel my heart rate increasing. I was not optimistic about the outcome, and a bit nervous about putting forward my case.

The Chairman asked me to take a seat.

"Why do you want to meet me?" he asked.

"Sir, I am Vijay Thariani. I had met you earlier, with Mr Gandhi."

"Yes, I remember. Go on."

"Sir, I developed a few health issues when I was on duty in Ahmedabad. Because of this, I will not be able to travel frequently outside of Bombay. About a month back or so, I sought a transfer out of the audit section, and if not possible, a reversion to clerical cadre, but have not heard anything from the Personnel Department. My probation period ends in three days. I have decided on reverting to the clerical cadre if I do not hear anything from the Personnel Department until the last day."

"Okay, anything else?" he asked tersely.

"Sir I am sorry to bother you for such a trivial matter at the last moment but I thought if you can help me out, I would be obliged."

"You are the son of retired officer Mr V.P. Thariani, right?"

"Yes, Sir."

"What are your thoughts on continuing as an Audit Officer if you do not have to travel?"

"Sir, it might create an ill feeling among fellow officers if special treatment is given to me."

He gave me a hard look. I looked down.

"Do you have a copy of the application given to Personnel?"

"Yes, Sir."

I gave him the copy.

"You can go now."

"Thank you, Sir."

I came out of his chamber and thanked his assistant. With a smiling face, in a low soft tone, she said, "Good luck."

I wondered what she was trying to convey as the Chairman did not give any hint, positive or negative, about what he would do with my request.

Right away, I went to see Mr Gandhi and brief him about my meeting with the Chairman. He said, "Son, I feel your work will be done. Good luck. Keep me posted."

I thanked him for his wishes.

By the next afternoon, I still had not heard anything. But I was relaxed. About an hour before I was to leave for the day, I got a call from HR instructing me to meet the HR manager immediately.

I went to see him. He asked me why I had gone to the Chairman directly and not tried to meet with him first. I told him, "Sorry sir, I had given my transfer/reversion application about a month ago but did not hear anything from the Department."

He looked upset. "How do you know the Chairman?"

I did not say a word and just smiled. He handed me the transfer order and asked me to report to the Chief Advances Manager the next day. He graciously wished me luck, adding, "Do not hesitate to meet me if you have any issues."

I was delighted. I was excited. I would continue to be an Officer but not in the audit department. It was nothing short of a miracle.

I went to inform Mr Gandhi. He welcomed me and said, "I think your work is done." I said, "Sir, your best wishes worked for me." He offered me a cup of tea. When we finished and I was getting up, he also got up and put his hand around my shoulder and said, "Son, always remember that you were bribed."

I decided that henceforth I would never wait for problems to disappear from my life by themselves, but make an attempt to directly address them.

CHAPTER THIRTY-TWO

The next day, I reported to the Advances Section as directed. Our section chief was visibly surprised that I was transferred from the audit section in less than 11 months, but thankfully he did not ask any uncomfortable questions. He assigned me to the Ledger area, where I was welcomed by my colleague sitting at the adjoining desk. I introduced myself and asked his name. He responded, "Sure, famous Gujarati humourist."

"Jyotindra Dave?" I asked.

We laughed and have remained friends ever since.

Davebhai was deeply involved in social work and was always eager to help someone if asked. He was resourceful too. I was inspired by him. He had a unique quality – if anyone asked him for help, he would say yes upfront only if he thought he could help, else he would politely decline. If he agreed, he would get fully involved in the matter until the work was accomplished. Even if he had said no, he would still try to seek a solution on his own, and if subsequently, he found one, he would pursue it for you. Jyotindra Dave was social work personified.

All through that day, I received calls from fellow audit officers all across the country asking the same question: "How did you manage the transfer?" I couldn't brief anyone about the circumstances which made my transfer possible. I, therefore, restricted myself to a one-line reply, "Last evening I got the transfer order."

Things were moving smoothly. I was enjoying my job and with the work-life balance in place was able to spend quality time with the family. One day, our ledger keeper brought to my notice that funds were insufficient in a particular account. The account holder happened to be the son of a government minister in office at that time. Upon reviewing the account, I found that on many occasions his account had gone into the red. After a few days, the debit was made good. He appeared to be a habitual defaulter, *albeit* temporarily. He never informed the concerned officers of the shortfall. Only after a few reminders, would he make the debit balance good.

I spoke to my departmental head, requesting him to speak with the account holder or permit me to speak with him. He warned me that because this was a sensitive account, we needed permission from the Chief Accountant. But he did not want to talk to him. On my insistence, he finally permitted me to talk to the Chief Accountant, "If you want to talk, go ahead, but do not refer to my name."

I went to the Chief Accountant, presented the facts, and convinced him about how badly the account was being conducted. "If we do not talk to him, he will consider that the bank is owned by him."

He gave me the go-ahead. I spoke to the customer, politely telling him that by clearing the cheque, his account would be overdrawn.

He was furious. Angrily he said, "I am instructing you to pass my cheque as was being done in the past two years." I somehow managed to control my temper. "I am sorry sir, but I will not be able to do so. I request you to bring in the required funds to the account within two hours. If not, I will be obliged to return your cheque."

He raised his voice. "Do you know who I am?"

"Yes, I know who you are. You are a customer and I am an officer of the bank calling you to inform you that your account has insufficient balance, and to let you know of the consequences if the required amount is not arranged for."

I could hear the sound of the phone being banged down. I immediately briefed my departmental head and the chief accountant about my conversation with the customer. Both of them said, "Good job."

I would later learn that both my immediate boss and his boss had instructed their assistants not to connect them with the customer should he call. He tried to talk to them but they were "unavailable".

After an hour or so, I received a call from the customer's assistant asking me not to return the cheque as they would arrange for the required amount to be credited to the account in half an hour. I thanked him for understanding. Thereafter, I do not recall needing to call that customer for a shortfall of funds, except maybe just once, but even then, at his request, I accommodated him by granting a temporary overdraft for a couple of days.

Days went by. My mother began talking to me about going to the Middle East in search of a job as the cost of living was going up in India. By now, my father, on his retirement, had taken up a position in UAE. He worked in a local bank, earning a good salary in terms of Indian rupees.

I was not keen, but as luck would have it, I got a hint that I might be transferred to Lucknow. Jaya and I discussed and deliberated. She convinced me to go to UAE to see what jobs were available. She reasoned that there was no downside because I already had a job in India.

I talked to my brother who organised a visitor's visa for me.

CHAPTER THIRTY-THREE

Before I proceed to discuss my journey to the UAE, I would like to share an unbelievable experience. While I was still a clerk, my friend Gul Shahani asked me if I had heard of Sai Baba of Shirdi. I hadn't. He asked me if I would be interested in going to Shirdi with him and another friend, Ashwin Dalal. The three of us decided to go but we were not aware of the route to get to Shirdi. All that we knew was that we had to go via Nasik.

I was assigned to the Fixed Deposit department immediately upon my return from the staff training college. Shahani had been in that department for many years. We soon became friends. In 1968, one day our officer introduced me to a new staff member and let me know that he would be working with me. I shook hands with him.

"I am Ashwin Dalal," he introduced himself.

"Are you a Gujarati?" I asked him.

"Yes," he said.

I suggested we speak in Gujarati and said, "*Chalo aapne canteen ma cha piva jaiye*," (Come, let us go to the canteen to have tea).

From that moment on we became friends.

Shahani and Ashwin both had a loving nature, were pure at heart, frank and transparent. We lost Shahani many years ago, but Ashwin and I are still in touch. We share a common birthday, though we were born in different years. I do not remember even a single incident when we argued on anything.

Ashwin's father was associated with a prestigious brokerage firm in the Bombay Stock Exchange. He introduced me to the firm's senior partner, Mr Mashruwalla, who was also vice president of the stock exchange at the time.

Mr Mashruwalla asked me, "Do you want to invest or just speculate?"

I did not know a thing about the stock market and responded, "A small investment and a little bit of speculation."

His corner office was in the old stock market building on the fifth floor. He called me to the window.

"What can you see down there?"

"People moving about."

"What else can you see?"

"A few parked cars."

"Good. Do you know who owns those cars?"

"No."

"All these cars belong to stockbrokers. None of these cars belong to their customers. Never speculate."

I followed his advice.

At lunchtime, the three of us went to the Tourism Office of the Maharashtra Government. We learnt that they conducted bus tours to Shirdi. We decided to visit Shirdi. For me, it was a good opportunity to spend time with friends. And so, while there, I did *darshan* without deep faith.

After about a month or so, Shahani asked me if we could go to Shirdi again as he had experienced some positive things happening in his life since our return. The three of us went again but this time opted to go by train. We completed the *darshan*, offered food to the poor and commenced our return journey late on a Sunday afternoon. At Kalyan Station, Shahani asked me whether I had started believing in Sai Baba or developed at least some faith in Him.

I carelessly said, "If this train halts at Ghatkopar station which is my destination (long-distance trains usually did not stop there), I will believe in Him." An elderly gentleman, overhearing my comments, interjected, "Son, you should not be talking like this about God." I was embarrassed and apologized.

Then the train stopped. Through the train window, we saw that it was a station. We thought it was Thane, the next scheduled stop after Kalyan. The train halted there for 10-15 minutes, which was unusual. We assumed it was due to a red signal. By now, we were restless as we were eager to reach home. I stood up from my seat, lifted the glass panel to lean out of the window to see what was happening. I saw something unbelievable. In the dim light, I read the sign 'Ghatkopar Station'. I shouted to my friends. "It is not Thane, we are at Ghatkopar Station. Give me my bag – I am getting down here."

I jumped out of the train and saw the green light flash. Someone commented, "It was a green light even when the train arrived at Ghatkopar Station. Not sure why it did not move for the last 10-15 minutes."

The moment I jumped out of the train, it started moving. Why did the train make an unscheduled halt for this long at the suburban Ghatkopar Station? I had no answer to this question except to tell myself that there would always be a conflict between the conscious and unconscious reasoning in one's mind.

CHAPTER THIRTY-FOUR

I reluctantly left for the UAE to look for a job. My brother was highly influential in Abu Dhabi. He asked me whether I was serious enough to work there. I responded that I would be fine only if my starting salary would allow me to stay independently with my family.

He said, "But we have a house here."

I replied, "What if I get a posting in a different Emirate such as Dubai or get transferred later on?"

He agreed that was an important consideration.

I told *Adha* and *Bha*, "I will wait for two months. If nothing acceptable happens, then I will go back to Bombay."

They did not like the fact that I was fixing a time limit because I had a record of going back from UAE to Bombay in three weeks.

Adha shortlisted three institutions – IMF, Central Bank of UAE and a UAE based International Bank. These institutions were considered good paymasters. He was trying hard to organize a meeting with certain senior employees of these banks but the outcome did not appear to be positive.

I was wait-listed for an interview with IMF and the one with the Central Bank of UAE was scheduled after two months. In the meanwhile, *Adha* was able to organize a meeting with the General Manager of the local International Bank through one of his doctor friends.

When I met with the General Manager, while he appeared to be satisfied with my 14 years of banking experience, he did have some specific questions.

"Have you ever worked in the Foreign Exchange Department?"

"No Sir, but I was in Audit, and attended the bank's training college then. So I have theoretical knowledge of the subject, but no practical experience. If I am selected and posted in the foreign exchange section, it will be like an interdepartmental transfer."

After a few more questions, he said, "You will get a call in a couple of days for a formal interview."

I thanked him and left.

When I got home after this meeting, I got a call from Jaya that a friend of mine in the Personnel Department of my bank in India had called to inform her that upon my return, I would have to report to the Lucknow Branch. She strongly suggested we try for the UAE rather than going to Lucknow. I agreed. The extent of how much change this meant for us was unknown. The only certainty was that life was about to change.

After two days, I received a call for a formal interview from the International Bank. During the wait, I had prepared myself with a focus on foreign exchange. At the interview, I saw the General Manager heading the interview panel sitting in the centre. On one side was the Head of HR and on the other, a local senior representative from HR. (I would learn of their positions only later).

The General Manager started by asking about my background, banking experience and just a couple of other basic questions. The UAE officer talked to the General Manager in Arabic, which I did not understand, but I heard words like Letter of Credit (LC). My immediate guess was he was asking him to test my knowledge of LC, which was a key instrument in the world of foreign exchange.

Knowing I had not worked in foreign exchange, rather reluctantly the General Manager asked me a question about LC. I answered his question elaborately. Seeing I was prepared, he went on to ask me a few technical questions about LC. I answered with confidence. The UAE officer appeared to be satisfied.

The HR head then asked me, "What is your current salary?" If I translated my current salary in rupees into the local UAE currency 'Dirhams (Dhs)', it would have worked out to around Dhs. 1,000. Instead of giving exact numbers, I said, "A little over four figures."

I was asked to leave. I thanked the panel. The General Manager instructed me to wait outside his office. I waited for about two hours. When he returned, he signalled me to join him. As soon as I sat, he said, "Look, I did not want to ask you any questions on LCs because you had informed me when you met me for the first time that you have not worked with LCs. But the situation was such that I had to ask you. You pleasantly surprised me by answering the technical questions correctly. How come?"

I responded, "Sir, I prepared thoroughly on the subject from a book that I had with me."

He said, "Until now, in most cases candidates referred to me by people known to me would say they know everything, and in the interview when I ask technical questions on a particular subject they let me down. I appreciate your honesty and effort."

I thanked him.

He asked me if I would be able to join immediately, in Dubai. I said, "Yes, Sir." He said, "Congratulations! You are selected. Go to HR in three days and collect your appointment letter."

I was excited and thanked him again. He wished me luck and said he would be available should I need his help anytime.

I was not able to fully correlate the emotions of my heart and mind. Both behaved as strangers. I came home. My father, brother, sister-in-law, nephew, niece were eagerly waiting to learn the outcome. Everyone congratulated me. I immediately called Bombay to break the news to Jaya, my mother and other family members.

My salary was yet unknown.

CHAPTER THIRTY-FIVE

After three days, I met Mr Fahad, a Pakistani national, from the HR team. He was the Personal Assistant to the chief of HR. He welcomed me and pulled out my appointment letter. It read – "Grade: E-1, Position: Clerk, Salary: Dhs. 6,230 per month. Posting at Dubai Branch".

I was surprised upon reading this and told Mr Fahad that the position of clerk was not acceptable to me as I was already an officer in a bank in India. He said, "Brother, over here, there is nothing like a clerk or officer until one gets a designated position. Unlike in our country, where the hierarchy in the bank begins with sepoy, clerk, officer and so on, in this country you will find that those in the cabins do all the work from typing, preparing vouchers, taking files to other tables and so on." He continued, "Take my case for example. I have been working here for the past 10 years. Even after that, at this time, I am in the same grade and salary as you are being offered. You are fortunate to get a good start. This is very rare. My advice to you is to accept this."

Even after this, I was not fully convinced. I asked him if I could use his telephone to call my brother. I shared the details of my appointment letter with *Adha*. He said, "Don't think twice. Just accept it."

I thanked Mr Fahad, accepted and acknowledged the appointment letter. Over the years, we became friends and kept in touch.

CHAPTER THIRTY-SIX

I was to join the Dubai branch of the bank the following Saturday. In the UAE the work week started the day after the weekly holiday on Friday. My father and brother came to drop me in Dubai on Friday. A temporary arrangement was made for my stay with my cousin, Pushpa, and her husband, Ashkaran. They graciously welcomed me and made me feel at home until I could rent an apartment in about three weeks.

Another cousin was also staying with us. On Saturday morning, he accompanied me to the branch on his way to work. I met the accountant Mr Ashraf Aziz and gave him my appointment letter. He asked me to wait for the manager and started asking me about my banking experience. I did not know the reason for his questions and I did not attempt to speculate.

After half an hour, the manager arrived. He was a fairly young man, looking smart in his black shirt and trousers. Mr Aziz introduced me and handed my appointment letter to him. They said something in Arabic that I did not follow. The manager shook hands with me and asked who had appointed me.

I was puzzled.

I replied, "Sir, I was interviewed in Abu Dhabi and was offered a posting in this branch."

"But who appointed you?" he inquired.

By now, I was thoroughly confused.

"Sir, I had applied for the position, was interviewed, got selected and asked to report here."

The manager appeared irritated and raising his voice slightly, again asked, "I'm asking who appointed you?"

I thought for a while and responded, "I am sorry sir. I do not understand your question."

Calming down, and now certain that I was as puzzled as he was, he said, "To whom did you give your application?"

"Sir, Mr Salah, the General Manager."

He asked, "Was he present during the interview?"

"Yes Sir."

Upon hearing this, he asked his secretary to connect him to Mr Salah. They spoke in Arabic. When he finished, his tone changed, and he said, "Welcome Mr Vijay. I will take you to the LC Department and introduce you to everyone there."

The staff of about 25 in the bank was noticeably surprised at seeing the manager taking me personally to the first floor where the LC Department was located. As we entered, the entire staff of the LC Department stood up. The manager introduced me to each one of them individually and asked me to meet him if I needed anything.

It was only later that I came to know that it was the first time that an appointment had been made at the head office and was then posted to a local branch. Until then, the hiring for the branch was all done locally.

The total staff strength was 10 in the LC section – seven Indians, two UAE nationals and one Palestinian. I again shook hands with everybody. After exchanging pleasantries, I was all set to start work.

The work environment was good even though the departmental head and his deputy were in the same grade and drawing the same salary as me. I realized then, that in the banking world, a lot depended on who you knew rather than who you were.

Jaya and the kids joined me in about 45 days by which time I had rented an apartment.

It is said that just like you cannot choose your family, you cannot choose your neighbours. If you get good neighbours it is akin to receiving God's blessing. This turned out to be so true in our case.

The D'Souza's – Martin and Elizabeth, and the Dayal's – Umesh and Nita, were two families that were God's precious gifts to us. We lived on the second floor of the building. Also coincidental was that our wedding anniversaries were on the 29th, although in different months.

Our relationship which began as neighbours soon developed into a close family friendship. I do not remember a single instance where we had even a minor dispute amongst us. Never in all the years that we have known them, have we had any misgivings towards each other. Our three families helped each other in all respects, and we were blessed to be able to understand each other's emotional and any other needs. We had two children each, so the six children grew up together as one family. It is not surprising that we continue to maintain the relationship, and are still as close to each other as we were in Dubai. I want to make a special mention of dearest Mihir, Umeshbhai and Nita Ben's son, and the youngest of the gang of six children. Though Mihir is no longer with us, he will always remain in our hearts and memories.

CHAPTER THIRTY-SEVEN

At the bank, we closed our books every fortnight (i.e. bi-weekly). It was not computerized as yet, and everything had to be done manually. On the day of balancing, everyone would typically eat lunch at the office instead of going home, leaving only when the work was completed. It was common in Dubai in those days to head home for lunch. Just as I was debating whether to do so, Mr Ashraf Aziz came upstairs and said "You Indians, all of you come down." Needless to say, I did not appreciate the tone of his voice. I was shocked. I asked the others how they tolerated this. The departmental head said that they had no option. Mr Aziz was always like that and if anyone confronted him, he was revengeful and made life difficult for the person.

At the branch, vegetarian and non-vegetarian food was offered combined. I, being a strict vegetarian, told Mr Aziz that I would be back in half an hour or so. He agreed. I went home, quickly had lunch, and returned to the branch. We sat down to balance the books and were able to complete the tasks quickly. As we were not allowed to leave the branch until every individual was done, we started talking. Because we had a common language, we were casually chatting in Hindi.

Mr Aziz came up as he heard us talk. He asked whether we had any problem balancing the books. When we said no, he responded, "Do not talk in Hindi, talk in English." Everyone was silent. Seeing no one respond, I said, "Sir, when we talk amongst ourselves we talk in Hindi. It is as natural as you talking in Arabic to other colleagues."

"I don't understand Hindi," he said.

I retorted, "We don't understand Arabic either."

"Arabic is the national language of this country." he shot back

"Sorry sir, but English is the official language of the bank." I countered.

He gave me an angry look and turned around. We heard a clear sound of thumping of feet as he stormed down. Everyone strongly suggested that I go down immediately and apologize to him else he would create problems for me. I did not say anything, leaving for the day without speaking to anyone except saying bye to Mr Aziz.

The next morning, he and I happened to meet outside the branch.

"Sir, I did not mean to hurt you yesterday."

"That's okay. I understood your viewpoint too."

I did not face any retribution but wondered whether he was the same person as everyone described to me or whether he was grossly misunderstood.

I had slowly started to establish myself in the branch. I was practically handling all the English correspondence for the managers. The branch was assigned its third manager in less than a year. I was also asked to handle the credit portfolio. My relationship with Mr Aziz had also evolved by now. While we would differ on some matters, we were able to discuss and amicably resolve those issues. Everyone at the branch was surprised at my cordial relationship with Mr Aziz despite the rocky start.

Soon after, we were on our fourth branch manager, Mr Samir Hassan. He was a close relative of the General Manager. While knowledgeable in banking affairs, he was not fluent in English. He was a good person at heart. We became friendly and he would sometimes share his family matters with me. He trusted me completely to the extent that he would sign any letter or memo drafted by me without any review or verification. I also took the utmost care to not misuse this trust and made sure that he understood exactly what was written. Sometimes he would suggest some changes which I would incorporate. Soon, I started getting recognition at the head office in Abu Dhabi.

A while later, a new CEO, Mr Greg Vory, was appointed to lead the bank. Within three days of taking over, he sent a memo to the branch expressing his desire to arrange a meeting with the top five credit clients of the branch. Everyone in the branch was excited. Two UAE nationals in the branch who were assisting me were keen to accompany the CEO to the client meetings. While not ideal, Mr Hassan could not say no to them. I arranged meetings with the clients but did not get to accompany the CEO, Branch Manager and the UAE nationals. My manager was worried given that I knew these clients the best. I reassured him that Mr Adil Rahman, one of the UAE nationals had good English speaking skills and was aware of the client's portfolio. That gentleman later went on to become Director-General of the Dubai Chamber of Commerce, and Ambassador of the country, the highest diplomatic post that any bureaucrat could aspire for.

The meetings took place as scheduled on the appointed day and time. After that was over, Mr Hassan called me to say he could not follow everything that the CEO spoke, but it appeared that everything went well. He also told me that every client inquired why Mr Vijay had not come. The CEO had asked who this Mr Vijay was. The manager explained to them that I was held up due to an urgent matter at the branch.

Two days later, Mr Hassan received a memo from the CEO asking to send call memos of his meetings with the clients. I suggested he ask Mr Rahman to write the call memos and offered to help him if needed. However, he wanted to wait to see whether the CEO remembered this before asking Mr Rahman. A day later, another memo was sent from the CEO's office. This time, he seemed annoyed. The letter was blunt – "Where are my call memos?"

Mr Hassan called me into his office. He said that he had spoken to Mr Rahman to write the memos but learnt that he was leaving early. He looked at me and said, "Now you write the memos!"

I did not respond. After a minute of silence, I told him, "Since I was not there, I do not know what transpired in the meeting. Even Mr Rahman told me that he could not follow the CEOs accent completely. So how can I randomly write something? Is it not proper to provide the CEO with an accurate description of what they discussed with the clients?"

While we were talking, we received a call from the CEO's Personal Assistant (PA). "He wants the memos on his table by Saturday morning."

Friday was a weekly holiday, and the manager, who by now was quite ruffled, simply said, "Vijay, you write whatever you can and want to write. The memos have to be sent today."

I reluctantly agreed, "Sir, okay. However, in the worst-case scenario, if this does not go well, it will not be my responsibility." He said, "Okay don't worry."

I started writing, recalling each client's needs and demands from the bank based on my periodic interaction with them. We were ready to dispatch the memos. The manager began reading them, but halfway down, just signed them and asked his assistant to send a van driver to drop the memos at the CEO's office in Abu Dhabi.

Early on Saturday morning, around 8:30 AM, the telephone operator informed me, "Vijay, the CEO wants to talk to you." I got a bit panicky. I asked the operator if she was sure that the CEO wanted to talk to me and not the manager. She answered in the affirmative stating that she had confirmed with his PA. She was now connecting the line. In my cabin, I stood up (out of the habit of respect to a senior officer).

"Good morning Sir, this is Vijay."

"Good morning. Did you write the call memos of my visit with branch clients?"

"Yes Sir, as I was instructed."

"But how could you do that when you were not even present?"

"Sir, I had no other option because my colleagues who were present could not give me a detailed briefing of your conversation with clients as they had already left for the day when we received your reminder to send the memos by Saturday morning. I am sorry Sir, but my writing was based on my experience with the clients and their needs, demands and expectations from the bank."

The CEO shared that what I had included in the memos was precisely the gist of his meetings with all the clients. He also shared his appreciation with me. Before he could disconnect the call, I asked, "Thank you sir, but how did you guess that I was the one who wrote these call memos?"

He answered, "Don't worry about that. Have a good day."

I was convinced common sense is not so common after all. It tends to betray us.

I ran to the manager and briefed him about my conversation with the CEO. Mr Hassan said, "He first called me on my direct number. Congratulations and thank you."

CHAPTER THIRTY-EIGHT

Soon after that incident, we had a new branch manager, whose appointment coincided with the visit of the Chief Advances Manager to all branches of the region in an exercise to weed out small and unprofitable accounts. Our branch manager asked me to prepare thoroughly which I started doing. We had about 120 borrowing accounts, not including term loans. I prepared a summary of all these accounts writing names of the partners, directors, key balance sheet numbers, financial ratios and profitability of each client with the branch.

Our branch was in the Northern Emirates, the largest of 10 branches in the region. The Chief Advances Manager, Mr Michael Lewis was to visit our branch the last. I was prepared for a marathon meeting as I had heard he was taking an average of two days per branch. My manager asked me to manage the show as he was not yet familiar with all the accounts. I had kept all client files handy in case we needed to refer to them.

Mr Lewis and his team arrived on the appointed date. I handed over the list of the accounts to him. He started asking for details of each account, what our experience with clients was, instructing us along the way which ones to mark for weeding out.

After about five hours, he realized that he had completed a review of all accounts without needing to refer to any file for details. He was surprised. He asked me, "Are we through with all the accounts?" I said yes. "How did you manage not to refer to any files? I showed him the summary sheet I was looking at when he inquired about specific numbers. Extending his hand to me he said, "I appreciate it. You saved me two days. Can you come to my hotel for coffee late afternoon, around 5 p.m.?

I accepted his invitation.

At exactly 5 p.m., I knocked on the door of his room. He invited me in. I found him to be a relaxed person with a friendly disposition, as opposed to his visit to the branch earlier that day where he had a perfect business-like attitude and attire.

We sat down. He casually conversed with me to find out about my background, banking experience, how I handled problematic customers, and some personal questions. While we were sipping coffee, he suddenly said, "Let me tell you something that you will not share with anyone."

I said, "Sure Sir."

"We are planning to reorganize all regions and are creating a post of Head of Regional Advances for each region with distinct identity and responsibility." He added, "As a matter of fact, the CEO himself asked me to see you and if satisfied, consider you for the newly created post. I am satisfied with you. I was thrilled at how swiftly we got through the accounts."

I was surprised and did not know how to respond. All that came out of my mouth was, "Thank you very much, Sir."

He then asked about my academics. He was surprised when he learned that I was not a commerce student but a graduate in literature and philosophy. I went on to share with him that I was judged the best Credit Analyst at a seminar organised in Dubai by a British consultancy firm in which representatives from all leading UAE banks participated.

"How did you manage all this?"

"Sir, determination."

"I am convinced you will be my first choice to head advances of your region but wait for the official communication. It will take about three to four months to finalize everything."

I realized there was no substitute for hard work and total commitment. It brings countless opportunities.

Very excited, I went home and shared the news with Jaya. "God is great", was her instant reaction.

CHAPTER THIRTY-NINE

Here again, I go back to yet another Believe It or Not experience.

I had now worked for a year and was due for my annual leave. At the time of accepting my appointment letter, Mr Fahad had informed me that I would be eligible for airfare for myself and my family to my home country, India.

I applied for leave as well as a travel claim. I submitted my application to Mr Aziz, our accountant. He said, "You will get family passage only from your second year on." He showed me a policy manual to this effect. It was clear and without any ambiguity. I requested him to forward my application to HR for their consideration. I told him what I had been verbally informed that I would be eligible from the first year when I had signed the appointment letter. He was adamant that he would not forward my application to HR. He was justified. While I was requesting him repeatedly to seek the decision of HR, our conversation became argumentative. Our manager came out of his office and asked what was going on. We told him. After patiently listening to both of us, he asked Mr Aziz to forward my application to HR for their decision. He did not like it that I was pushing back, and rightly so. I also began thinking as to why I was so insistent when the manual was clear.

When I got home, I told Jaya about the incident. I do not hesitate to say even now that perhaps I was in the wrong. While eating lunch, I told Jaya, "You always talk of your Mataji (who was already instrumental in curing me of my 5 p.m. phobia through her blessings). Let us see if we get family passage. If it is positive for us, I will have even more faith in her."

Childish thinking and demand once again. You could even consider it to be a bit arrogant. I don't think Jaya appreciated this statement, so she simply said, "I have full faith in Her."

Two days later, the branch received an approval memo from HR granting family passage. When Mr Aziz handed over a copy of the approval to me, it was apparent that he was not happy. Word went around the branch that I was highly influential.

I could not figure out if this approval was due to divine blessings or influence (knowing the General Manager) or an error on the part of HR. Nonetheless, I resolved to henceforth enter into only logical arguments that have sustainability.

CHAPTER FORTY

Meanwhile, my father had retired from the bank in the UAE and had returned to Mumbai. When I returned from my leave, I found our branch had yet another manager, the sixth one. He was an Indian national who had recently retired from a nationalized bank in India. We got along well.

Any credit proposal sent by our branch to the head office was met with much appreciation. One such presentation was even kept at the bank's training college as a sample. I was happy and satisfied as was my manager with me.

By now the bank had started working on retrenchment to cut costs, without being concerned about the nationality of the employee. Many people lost their jobs. Everyone was anxious and worried. I was not an exception.

One morning, when I went to the manager's cabin I saw the name of our telephone operator on his writing pad. She was an Indian national.

After finishing my work with him, I casually asked him, "Why is this name written on your writing pad?"

He made me close the door and said, "We have to recommend a name for a golden handshake. I have her in mind."

"Because she is Indian?"

He nodded.

"Sir, can I name at least three others who in my opinion are good for nothing? But they are not Indians. Ms Bhairavi Naik, the telephone operator is not only performing the duties of a telephone operator, but she also manages incoming and outgoing mail, typing of LCs, and other important work. What's even better is that she performs all these additional duties efficiently, always with a smile on her face. Why is she being recommended?"

He said the Regional Manager, Mr Pawan Bansal, also an Indian national, had asked for one name, preferably an Indian, so that nobody would accuse us of favouring Indians.

I was shocked. I protested, "Sir, in my view, this is a gross injustice. This is not correct. We should suggest a name based on performance and not based on nationality."

He responded, "I am relatively new and helpless as I am under instructions from Mr Bansal."

I was disturbed, angry, and agitated.

"Sir, I have a suggestion…"

"It is of no use, Mr Bansal has made up his mind. I have no problem if you want to talk to him to change his mind."

"Sir, this will not be proper. It will send the wrong signal that you are unable to make a decision."

He stared at me, "Okay then, what is your suggestion?"

"I suggest you send four names in the order that you feel appropriate. Next to each name, write the job description and the annual appraisal grade for at least three years."

He immediately instructed his assistant to not send any earlier memos drafted by him recommending the telephone operator's name. He asked me to draft a letter to HR, which I did. He signed the letter and sent it to the Regional Manager.

The next day the manager received a call from Mr Bansal who inquired from him why he made such a recommendation instead of sending just one name. My manager told him that it was my suggestion and that he agreed with me.

As I was informed, with little hesitation and annoyance, Mr Bansal had forwarded this list to HR along with his recommendations of which we were unaware. We later learnt that HR picked the first name that we had written, who was also our weakest performer. Ms Naik's job was saved and she deserved it.

About 22 years after I had resigned and left the UAE, when I was visiting for a few days, I went to the bank. Ms Naik was still there. She recognized me. I did too.

"You are still here?" I asked.

She was in tears.

"It is because of you Vijay. You did not even tell me anything about how you managed to save my job when I invited you to my house for dinner before you went back to India for good. It was the manager's secretary who told me how you did it even risking the wrath of the Regional Manager. She told me this when she was leaving UAE for good."

I told her, "Bhairavi, I have not done you any favour. I did what I found appropriate at that time and in the interest of the bank." But her eyes were teary when I left.

CHAPTER FORTY-ONE

One day, the Chief Advances Manager, Mr Michael Lewis, called to inform me that I would be assigned to another branch in a few days. This branch would be designated as the regional office temporarily. He also said that there would be a circular designating me as Head of Advances in a few months but asked me to not share the information with anyone.

Before I moved to the other branch, the manager said, "Vijay, I am sending a recruit to you. Please talk to him and tell me what work can be assigned to him."

In a few minutes, a gentleman came up to my office, wearing a formal suit. I greeted him and asked him to sit while I completed what I was doing. When I finished, I got up, shook hands with him, and asked him his name. "Hamid Taylor," he said. I told him that I had heard the name Hamid Taylor, the manager of a branch of a neighbouring bank. Hamidbhai (as I would call him since) said that he was the same person and asked me my name.

"Vijay Thariani."

"I know one Mr Thariani who worked in a bank in India. Are you related to him?"

Smiling, I said, "I am his son. I was also working in the same bank."

Hamidbhai said, "I was also working in the bank where your father was a senior officer in the HR department."

I liked him immediately. I got up and sat next to him. I gathered that he was appointed in a grade and salary much higher than mine. But from that moment onwards, we became friends, and also family friends. I have no hesitation to say that I have learned a lot from him. He was what I would describe as a model banker. But even more than that he is one of the finest, loving, and most noble human beings.

To date, we have maintained excellent brotherly relations. I do not know if, through my book, my words will be enough to describe his nobility. The same goes for his wife, Najmabhabhi.

Hamidbhai and Najmabhabhi always believed that we desperately need brotherhood and understanding. Religion is a private affair between an individual and God. Religion should bind each other and not divide.

Our brotherly relationship is a great example to support this view and belief.

Both our families whole-heartedly participated in the weddings of our respective children. I still fondly remember, at Rachit's wedding, how they were dancing as members of the Baraat Group. We cherish these memories.

The best part of our relationship is that we never had to put any effort to maintain it.

CHAPTER FORTY-TWO

As planned, I moved to the other branch in the credit department, before I moved to the permanent regional office.

I knew the manager. In a few days, I was surprised to find that the quarterly returns to the head office were never sent on time. I resolved that would not happen while I was responsible. The next quarter was to end in a fortnight. I worked hard on the preparation of the credit returns alone. The report was ready for dispatch on time. Just as I was contemplating whether my effort had been worth it, I realized that the Sectional Head, Mr Habibullah, who had to sign the reports, had gone out. Nobody knew whether he would be coming back to the branch.

I had no choice but to go to the manager and explain the situation. I asked the manager whether he could sign the returns, and then, for the first time, the branch would be on time. The manager appreciated this and agreed with me. He signed them and sent them for dispatch.

Just a few minutes before closing, Mr Habibullah, came back. I presume someone informed him that I was sending the returns with the manager's signature.

He seemed disturbed. As I was preparing to leave for the day, I found a memo on my table addressed to me: "Vijay, you have insulted me by not taking my signature on reports. Please explain."

We sat just across from each other, yet he chose to put this in writing, and not just that, copied various department heads including Mr Lewis and the HR department. For a moment, I was unsure what to do. Then I replied, copying the same people he had, "Dear Mr Habibullah, I have no intention whatsoever to bypass you or your authority. I talked to the manager who agreed to sign in your absence as no one in the department had a clue of when you were to return to the branch. Moreover, this is the first time that the returns were sent to head office before the deadline. Please note that my actions today were in the best interest of the branch and by no means meant to be an insult to you. Hope you will understand my approach."

My colleagues knew about this incident and were waiting to see what would happen.

Mr Habibullah looked at me before leaving but did not say anything.

Then, I got a call from the dispatch clerk to check if he should send my reply. I asked him whether Mr Habibullah had asked him to not send the memo. He replied in the negative. But he also warned me that Mr Habibullah was close to the ruling family and the

Chairman of the bank. I knew he was saying this to discourage me from sending my response.

I thanked him for the information but asked him to send it anyway. I went to the manager, showed him what Mr Habibullah had written and my response. He simply said, "Let's see what happens. Don't worry."

Then, as promised, in a few months, we received a circular from Mr Lewis's office describing the creation of various regions and the newly created position of the Regional Head of Advances. My name figured there in reading – Vijay Thariani, Head of Regional Advances, Northern Emirates.

At least three of my previous branch managers would be now reporting to me for their credit portfolios.

The manager received the circular first, came to my office and said, "Vijay, congratulations! You deserve it." I could not say anything beyond, "Thank you."

Behind him was Habibullah. He hugged me warmly and said, "Vijay, a thousand congratulations." I said, "Mr Habibullah, thanks. I look forward to your cooperation."

After that incident, until the time I was in the bank, we did not have any confrontations.

As my colleagues congratulated me one by one, Mr Bansal also did so saying that it was the result of my hard work. I found myself thinking that this was an unexpected opportunity. It was now up to me how I converted it, with logic and rationale, into a successful endeavour. Only if I was able to do that, would I be able to prove to myself that I had notable leadership qualities. Luck can help someone only so far. One has to consistently perform and prove oneself deserving of opportunities.

Before I assumed my new role, our American CEO was replaced with a British CEO, Jim Chambers.

CHAPTER FORTY-THREE

I moved into my new office. It was in the same branch. My cabin was next to Mr Bansal's. We had a common secretary. I was also appointed on the Credit Committee of the region with immediate effect with the second signature right (ability to sign a document to authorize spending).

I spent the next seven days getting familiarized with the new job and its duties. We had 10 branches in the region. Originally, the branch correspondence was sent by telex or fax or delivered by hand. In the seven days, I was able to design and adopt certain procedures of my own that would allow us to get a quick decision on credit proposals. As a matter of habit, I would not keep any matter unattended before I left for the day.

Since I did not have any discretionary powers yet (the ability to sanction a loan without further approval), I would analyse the proposal and send it to the Regional Manager with my recommendations for his consideration and signature. He was pleased with my approach and analysis and was generous in saying that I had exceptional analytical skills and an enquiring mind. Although I knew that I was just doing my job, the appreciation was encouraging, considering that he used it sparingly.

One day, Mr Chambers sent a memo to the regional office notifying us that he would visit us at 8 a.m. on a certain day. Our Regional Manager instructed everyone in the Regional Office and branch to be on duty latest by 7:30 a.m.

My secretary and I were always in the office between 7:30 and 7:45 a.m. On the day of his anticipated arrival, we reached the office before 7:30 a.m. I had a routine which was to go to my office, and before starting work, have a cup of tea and plan my workday. My secretary knew that I would not attend to any calls during this time.

Exactly at 8 a.m. when I was in the middle of something, my secretary called to inform me that there was someone who wanted to see me. I asked her to have the person wait for five minutes. Mr Bansal was not in office as yet. After five minutes I called and asked the secretary whether the visitor was a customer or was he the CEO? She paused and said that he did not look like a CEO but she would ask him. After a couple of seconds, looking completely flustered, she ran into my cabin and said, "Sir, it is Mr Jim Chambers, the CEO!"

I immediately went outside. I saw a man who looked around 60, dressed simply in a jacket, but wearing no tie. He had a small hand pouch about the size of a flat lunch box, looking no different than any other working professional.

I apologized for making him wait. As we entered my cabin, I offered my chair to him. He shook his head and said a firm 'No', telling me that it was my cabin, so I should be sitting there. I asked him if he would like a cup of tea or coffee. He refused and said politely that he was at the hotel next door and had just finished breakfast.

I said, "Sir, Mr Bansal should be here any minute." He surprised me by saying, "I have come to meet you." He asked me several questions – about my experience, my time with regional advances etc. I could sense him watching me closely, not just my answers to his questions, but also the attitude and confidence of my tone.

After a few minutes, our conversation became more relaxed. I found that he had 37 years of experience with global banks. He requested some coffee. I had asked the secretary to inform me when Mr Bansal comes in. Around 8.30 a.m. she informed me that Mr Bansal had arrived. I told Mr Chambers. He said, "Let us finish here first." I asked my secretary to inform Mr Bansal that the CEO would see him in a while.

Over the next several minutes, our discussion became so friendly that I almost forgot that I was talking to the CEO of my bank. I could hear someone pacing the floor outside my cabin. It was Mr Bansal, I was sure.

After almost an hour, Mr Chambers questioned me. "Vijay, what do you think of before you approve any loan?"

I replied without any hesitation, "I ask myself if it was my money, would I lend it to this client?"

Mr Chambers looked pleased. He held out his hand and said, "I do precisely the same thing."

I escorted him to Mr Bansal's cabin and asked my secretary to inform me as soon as he left. In just about 10 minutes I got a call from my secretary that he had left. I was a bit surprised. Before I could even get up from my chair, Mr Bansal flung open my cabin door, came inside and closed it. In one breath, looking visibly disturbed, he said, "Jim Chambers did not wait any longer as he had to travel to Sharjah. Can you brief me on what he talked to you about for an hour or so?" I briefed him about everything, except Mr Chambers' last question, my response to it and his reaction to my response.

Three days after the visit, I was granted discretionary powers aggregating to Dhs. 3 Million. Mr Bansal joked, "It appears that the CEO had just come to meet you. Congratulations!" I picked up the phone and thanked the CEO. He just said, "Congratulations, good luck."

CHAPTER FORTY-FOUR

Before telling you any more about my career journey, I want to share with you my experience of listening to my conscience and following my sixth sense.

While I was in my first branch, we had a client, M/s WE Enterprises. Mr Rajesh Advani was the sole proprietor. I had an excellent relationship with him. I had even sought his help in getting visit visas for my brother-in-law and sister-in-law.

He was considered a good customer. At every annual review, he would ask for an increase in his credit facilities. I would not allow it but would request him to increase his fixed deposits linked to his borrowing account as security to enable me to recommend an increase in facilities to the Head Office. For some reason, I was always hesitant in giving him any more credit than he already had with the bank.

After I moved to Regional Advances as its Head, at one of the social parties I saw Mr Advani and Mr Bansal having a drink and chatting. I always knew Mr Advani was street smart and was cosying up to avail the facilities.

As expected, and anticipated, I received a call early next morning from Mr Bansal's office.

"Vijay, how is Advani?"

"Who Advani?" I asked feigning ignorance.

"Proprietor of M/s WE Enterprises."

"Good," I responded.

"How is his account operation?" he asked.

"Satisfactory."

"Balance Sheet?"

"Good."

"Last evening at the party, you must have seen that I was talking to him. He was complaining that on many occasions he had asked for an increase in facilities but without result. I do not remember you even recommending that."

"That is correct, Sir," I responded.

"Why? Any reason?" he asked.

I responded at length, "Sir, M/s WE Enterprises is a sole proprietary concern. On three or four occasions I requested Mr Advani to induct at least one of his family members and make it a partnership concern. His wife, brother, father are with him in Dubai and that should be easy for him to do. Also, when he travels outside the country, and we receive shipping documents in his absence, he calls and asks me to release them with a promise to sign them upon his return to Dubai. I have obliged him at least thrice. But now, I am not comfortable continuing this practice. I have also been requesting that he gives at least a specific power of attorney to any of his family members even if he does not want to create a partnership. Once, he jocularly told me that he was not doing that as in case he wanted to default on his debts and flee the country – it would be easy. This made me uncomfortable. After this, with great difficulty, I convinced him to make someone like his father-in-law, a prominent businessman in Dubai as a guarantor for M/s WE Enterprises. Currently, his account status is his personal guarantee, personal guarantee of his father-in-law and our risk for the credit is covered by 30% in the form of deposit under lien with us."

Mr Bansal was listening attentively. "So, what is the hesitation now?"

"What I have a problem with, is his suspect intentions."

"Look, Vijay, we cannot do banking on hypothetical apprehensions. Prepare a proposal granting increased limits to Mr Advani."

Knowing that I could not convince him, I simply said, "Okay, Sir."

I prepared a proposal with an increased limit that would be beyond my discretionary powers but within the discretionary powers of the Regional Manager. However, I did not recommend increasing limits. Instead, I gave my reasons for not recommending and summed up by noting, 'Due to suspect intentions of the client, I do not recommend proposed increase until such time these limits are substantially covered by tangible securities'.

Upon reading my recommendation, Mr Bansal was displeased and very angry. He tried to convince me to change my negative recommendations. But I stood my ground and told him that my conscience would not permit me to do so and if it were my own money, I would not lend it to M/s WE Enterprises. The words I said to Mr Chambers came back to me at that time.

Sensing that I would not budge, he asked me to revise the proposal, with an even higher limit, slightly more than his discretionary powers, so that the proposal had to go to the head office. I did that but retained my recommendation. He overrode that with a single sentence: "Do not agree with Head of Regional Advances. I recommend."

The next day I received a call from Mr Amin, Head of Credit Facilities in the Head office. He seemed irritated and asked me why my view differed from that of my superior. I explained my reasons to him. This annoyed him further and he warned me that disagreeing with my manager, would not be good. I stood firm and told him that my conscience did not permit me to do that. He realized that he could not change my mind, and banged down the phone.

I was unperturbed. My intuition was telling me that I was right.

The following day, I received yet another call, this time from Mr Lewis. He asked me the same question and why I was differing from the Regional Manager. I once again politely explained my reasons.

"Are you sure about what you have written?" he asked

"Yes, Sir." I confidently responded.

"This is an unusual situation which is alien to the culture of the bank," he said.

"Sir, with due respect, either you or any of my superiors can override my recommendation," I respectfully countered.

"Then why has this file come to me? The proposal is within the power of Amin."

"I am not sure."

"Let me see what I have to do. If needed I will get in touch with you."

"Sure sir, thank you."

After two days Mr Lewis again called me. He said that he had discussed the matter with the CEO and that they had sent back the package to Mr Amin to deal with the case on its merits. He paused and continued, "Vijay, the CEO appreciated your stand."

I was relieved by Mr Lewis's call, although I wondered why he called me. There was no reason for him to inform me. I then realized that he perhaps had a soft corner for me.

Mr Amin approved to increase the limit as recommended by Mr Bansal, turning a blind eye to my recommendation.

Before the next annual review for this client, I resigned and left Dubai for good.

Almost a year or so after I was back in Mumbai, Hamidbhai called me.

"Vijay, everyone was thinking of you at the bank today. Rajesh Advani fled from the UAE without repaying his debts to the bank."

All I could say was, "It is unfortunate that it happened."

"No, the CEO has viewed this very seriously. He is asking Bansal and Amin why they could not assess the client's integrity if their subordinate was able to do so. And their attention was drawn to it with reasons. Especially when they had ample opportunity on social occasions to gather information on clients. Why did they fail?"

After a couple of months, I got the news that both Mr Bansal and Mr Amin were asked to resign. The reasons might have been many, but I felt that one of them was this incident. I felt sorry for Mr Bansal, who otherwise was a kind-hearted man. He always appreciated my work, except on this one occasion.

One more incident comes to mind, where vision and foresight were at play, but it was not until much later that people realized it.

Before I moved to the regional office, I was entrusted with a job to identify a new location for the branch mainly due to traffic congestion in the area and for bigger premises to facilitate expansion. I was able to prepare a report on the relocation of the bank within a fortnight.

I did my due diligence and suggested moving away from our existing location. The new place I identified was on the street which did not have any commercial buildings except for a small representative office of a Dutch bank.

In support of my identifying the street, I stated my reasons –

Dubai was expanding horizontally.

The elite class of Dubai was already located (including our existing clients), and moving to that side.

The landlord had come to the bank to ask for a loan. He wanted us to finance his upcoming multi-story building. I felt that if we could finance him, we could have him adjust a certain percentage of the rental against his loan instalment.

If we decided to move there, we would be the first full-fledged bank branch on the street that was two to three km long. Being first came with its advantages.

This street has the potential to become a hub of banking activities and corporate offices, as everyone was looking for solutions like we were, to the parking problem.

This site was a three-minute driving distance and 10 minutes walking distance from our existing branch.

One day the street will be known as Bank Street.

Everyone agreed at the branch level. A detailed proposal with projections was sent to the Head Office. Mr Richard Baron, the acting Regional Manager, came to the branch to discuss the proposal further. He appeared to be satisfied with my answers. Before leaving, he said that they would finalize and let us know the decision within two days. For some reason, I felt that he was not happy.

After a few days, we received a decision – "Look for alternatives". I was disappointed. As I had not been a part of the decision-making process, I did not know of the reasons why they did not go with our recommendation.

Shortly thereafter, we moved to another location nearby. On a visit to Dubai a few years after I had left, I found that the branch had moved to the same street which I had originally recommended.

Even more satisfying was that this street is now popularly known as Bank Street as I had originally predicted.

CHAPTER FORTY-FIVE

I now come back to the point from which I took a detour.

Our daughter Rachana was already in eighth grade and our son Rachit in fifth grade. At that time in the UAE, education was available only up to twelfth grade, so we needed to be sure we had a plan for their further studies.

As we thought about the future, Jaya and I narrowed down on three options:

1. Continue to work in Dubai, let children finish their studies up to whatever grade was available then take a call depending on circumstances.

2. Leave the children with one set of grandparents back in India. We continue staying in Dubai.

3. Resign from the job and all of us go back to Mumbai for good.

We discussed the pros and cons of all three options. Option 1 would lead us to the same circumstances as we were facing today. Option 2 would not be a good idea as my parents were ageing. My in-laws were younger, but soon all their children would be ready to settle down in life. Therefore, we decided to opt for option 3 – leave Dubai for good and return to Mumbai.

But the question was, what would we do in India to generate a regular source of income? We could not figure anything out for a few months. But as luck would have it...

Jaya's parents were engaged in an independent jewellery business. Before we migrated to the UAE, they had opened a store in Mumbai's main jewellers' street. Jaya's younger brother, Jaggi, visited the UAE, just as we had decided to return to India for good.

At the dinner table, he informed us of their plans to expand and that they were thinking of bigger retail premises on the same street. Without suggesting anything, I informed him about our decision to leave the UAE, sharing our reasons for the same. He casually asked, "Can you join us?"

I told him that I had not decided anything as yet about my plans upon returning to India.

"However, you may discuss this with other family members. I will also think it over," I said.

For the rest of his holiday with us, we went sightseeing, on social visits and so on. We did not discuss this matter again.

After he left, Jaya and I discussed his proposal.

"Jaya, can we join them if they all agree?"

She asked, "Are you for it?"

"I think so," I responded.

"You don't know anything about the jewellery business. And initially, perhaps even for a considerable time, you will be fully dependent on them to understand all aspects of this business."

"Whatever I know of them, they will educate and train me in the tricks of the trade. From my side, I will do my best and learn the business as quickly as possible. I will not let them down or become a burden to them."

She said, "I think we should do something on our own."

I was surprised, "Why are you so apprehensive? It is almost 18 years since we got engaged and I do not remember even a single instance where we might have had any heated or unnecessary argument."

She was frank. "Business is different from personal relations. I'm not in favour of doing joint business."

I tried to reason with her, "Look, we have limited resources to invest in a business of our own. They are in favour of me joining them, we can invest in property (shop) in equal ratio. So, we will not feel fully obligated even though I will surely carry some sense of obligation."

"To be under someone's obligation is not in your nature."

"I fully understand that. Even though it will be a little difficult for me, I will have to compromise somewhere to do something. Here, without any gestation period, we will have some regular income."

"I still have my reservations. I have seen and you will agree that generally, family partnership business ends in family feuds."

"I am promising you, I will never mix family relations and business matters."

"If you are so convinced and confident, then I am okay. But do not blame me if things do not go the way you foresee."

She was unhappy and agreed to the business proposal with reluctance. For a moment, even I was shaken. Eventually, I resolved from within – "I will, I can."

After a month or so, I sent them a message of my readiness to join their partnership business.

I told Jaya, "Every end is a new beginning."

CHAPTER FORTY-SIX

Happy, but not really excited, I went to India for a week to discuss with my to-be partners and family members before making a final decision.

I was warmly welcomed as usual.

We discussed setting up another independent outlet in the suburbs away from the existing location in the main market, but the head of the family, Shri Bhagwandas Kesaria (*Dada* as we affectionately called him) was not interested. He had decided on bigger shop premises just a building away from their existing business place.

After two days, I suggested we sit and finalize the terms of the partnership and take a final call if we choose to move ahead. *Dada*, my three brothers-in-law (Abu, Suresh and Jaggi) and I had a closed-door meeting at their residence. Most of the conversation was between *Dada* and me, with the others keenly observing and listening. While *Dada* was talking decisively, I was not aware if he had already consulted his sons. I was talking to all of them and my gestures were such that I was addressing them jointly and individually.

"I have come to know that you have a concrete proposal," I began.

Dada confirmed, "Yes, we have identified a shop in a building which is just two buildings away from our current shop."

"Before we get down to broad modalities, I want to know if all of you and other family members are also in agreement with my becoming part of your business," I continued.

"Yes, we have talked over it and we are agreeable."

"Good to know this. So how do we proceed?"

"We first buy the premises."

"What will be the size of the investment?"

"Do not worry about that at this stage."

"No, I want to know how much I need to invest only then will I decide if I want to join."

"OK, we will have four partners, my three sons and you will have an equal share. Your share will be 25%."

"What about the size of the investment?"

Dada mentioned the amount towards the purchase of the shop.

I said, "OK, I will invest 25% of the total cost of buying the shop. But we should have five shares."

"Five? Why?"

"We will have one share for you, plus the three shares collectively of your sons, and one of mine. But, I will contribute 25% as my investment."

"Why?" he asked in puzzlement.

I said, "It is your creation. You have established this business with your hard work. You are the architect."

"So are you saying you will contribute 25% towards the value of the shop and we will still have five shares in profit and loss?"

"Yes, I prefer that. I will also not claim any stake in the stock, because I will not be able to contribute to stock value even proportionately. So, we can agree that I will remain a profit and loss sharing partner at 20% +25% share in shop premises."

Everyone agreed.

Dada suggested changing the name of the company to reflect my addition – from ending with 'and sons' to 'and company'.

I immediately said, "This is not required. It is the brand name. Also, if anyone has to leave the partnership, it will be me. Let your family name continue for generations with this family business."

After some more discussion, we agreed to continue with the existing name.

Dada asked, "Is there anything else that we need to talk over?"

I asked, "Do we need to make a partnership agreement?"

He answered, "Yes, I will take care of that. We will purchase a shop in the name of the company and as advised by our chartered accountant."

"So, shall I go ahead and apply for RBI permission? It is required if any NRI wishes to invest in India."

"Sure, go ahead."

"OK thank you, and I will try my best to contribute towards the progress of the business."

On my flight back to Dubai, I was contemplating whether I had faltered anywhere in the discussion of finalizing terms. I told myself, "No, you have done what is just and fair." Yet, I was anxious to share the decision with Jaya. The only thing that made me nervous was that she was not happy with me doing business with close relatives. I tried to console myself thinking I would reassure her that should anything happen in the business that would pose a threat to any relationship, I would abide by what I had promised to her.

CHAPTER FORTY-SEVEN

I briefed Jaya about what we had decided. She said, "I am still not convinced."

For the first time, without mincing words, she said, "Think again. I know you are aware that my father was in a partnership with other family members before this, which did not end well. You played an active role in pacifying him and convincing him not to resort to legal action. Relations between our families were at the lowest level. I am worried about that. All I want to tell you is that I know you as much as I know my father and my brothers."

Her voice was choked with emotion.

I remained silent.

After a pause, she continued, "You know that we are investing all our savings. God forbid if any adverse situation arises, how are you going to manage it? I trust you and I trust my father and brothers. But I have also seen one of the sweetest relationships turning into one of the bitterest."

I suggested we talk it over the next day.

The next day, I tried to reassure her, "Look, I understand your worry and fear. Let us leave it to God to shape our future. I trust them, and from my side, I assure you that I will not ditch them. If for whatever reason, something goes wrong, I will not involve you in our differences or disputes. I feel at this stage you are concerned as you have experienced such unpleasant situations in the past. It is natural. Once again, I am promising you, I will never mix family relations and business matters."

I only prayed to God to give me enough strength to abide by my promises if such a situation arose.

The deal for the purchase of the shop was done. I had to obtain RBI permission as NRIs were then required to do for any investment in India. This was done way ahead of my sending the promised investment funds. I sent my cheque for 25% of the shop's value immediately. We also arranged for school admission for the children. Since the school term had already started, we arranged for both children to stay with their grandparents. They were happy with their uncles and aunts. And we were preparing to call it a day in the UAE.

The furnishing of the shop had commenced. I sent some photographs of jewellery shops in the UAE. While we were checking each day off, I was informed that basic furniture frames were ready and only finishing touches like lamination was required.

I reconfirmed with *Dada* whether there were any second thoughts about the joint venture as I had to resign from my job giving a notice of at least 30 days. He asked me to go ahead and gave a tentative date by which the shop would be open. I asked him whether I should wait until everything was ready and then resign during the waiting period. He was loud and clear in saying that our partnership would start the day I arrived in India. And if there was a delay for any unforeseen reason, he asked me to come to the existing shop to learn. I asked him, "Learning is fine, but since the business in which I am investing has not even started, how can I be a partner from the date of my arrival in India?" He replied, "When I say business, I mean our existing business irrespective of the fact how many outlets we have."

"Thank you for clarifying," I said.

I prepared to resign.

CHAPTER FORTY-EIGHT

Jaya and I worked out our date of departure from the UAE. Since my Regional Manager was on leave, I submitted my resignation letter directly to the Head Office. Only Hamidbhai knew about it. The next day, the Chief Advances Manager, Mr Lewis, called me and asked me in surprise, "Vijay, what is this resignation letter! Are you serious?"

I replied, "Yes, Sir. I am serious."

"Why did you not share your intention to resign verbally with me before putting it in writing?"

"I am sorry Sir. But I thought that if I had spoken to you about it before, you may have been able to convince me to not leave."

"So why do you think I will not be able to convince you now?"

I was calm when I answered, "I am sorry Sir, but I do request you to accept my resignation."

He asked me, "What is the real reason for this?"

I replied honestly, "Sir, I have taken into account three compelling reasons. One, education in this country is only until Grade 12. My daughter is already in Grade 9. I do not want to leave my children in India alone. Two, my parents are getting older. I do not want to burden them or my in-laws with extra responsibility for my children if I send them to India to study. Three, it has been my dream to own a business someday. I am leaving to pursue this dream."

He paused for a bit and then asked, "OK, but I have one question and expect an honest answer. Are you planning to join any other bank or institution in UAE for a better position or pay?"

I replied, "No Sir. That thought has never crossed my mind."

He went on, "I am disturbed. I cannot digest this right now. I will talk to you later about this. In the meanwhile, please reconsider your decision."

I apologized, "I am sorry sir. But I do not think my decision will change."

After I hung up, I was also a bit disturbed.

I immediately called Hamidbhai to brief him of my conversation with Mr Lewis. He fully understood my reasons and appreciated my decision when I first broke the news to him. When I came home for lunch, I told Jaya about my conversation with Mr Lewis. She knew him by name and the fact that he was responsible for elevating me to my current position. She only said, "We still have time to think about it."

I was silent.

That night, I tossed and turned, getting no sleep at all.

The next morning when I was ready to go to the office, Jaya said, "You look disturbed. Just relax. I am with you and will support any decision that you take."

That made me feel a bit better.

I reached the office earlier than usual. My secretary, Flavia, realized something was wrong and inquired whether I was feeling unwell. My face has always been the index of my heart, and for people who know me, it is sometimes easy to read my moods through my face.

As soon as the bank opened, our General Manager, Mr Dan Langer called me. He was American.

"Good morning, Vijay."

"Good morning, Sir."

"How are you doing?"

"I am fine."

"Are you sure?"

"Sir, did Mr Michael Lewis speak to you?"

"Yes. You know my reason for my call today."

"Yes, Sir."

"Michael told me about your resignation and reasons. I do not want to delve into the merits of the reasons, but do you mind repeating them for me?"

I told him exactly what I had told Mr Lewis.

"Hmm. I am disappointed. When Michael, who is more disappointed than me, and I were thinking of restructuring the regions, your name was the first in line for Head of Regional Advances – Northern Emirates. We are happy with your performance."

"Thank you, Sir."

"Why did you not wait for your Regional Manager to return from his leave?"

"Sir, the reason is the same as why I did not talk to you before providing the letter. I was afraid of being convinced to change my decision."

"Have you done your homework thoroughly? Do you have experience in the business that you are getting into?"

"No Sir, I do not have any experience. But I am banking on my close relatives, with whom I am partnering, to teach me."

"And if you don't mind, can you tell me which business you intend to join?"

"It's a family jewellery business."

"That's great. But in my opinion, it is not a great idea to start a joint venture in which you have zero experience."

"Thank you for your feedback, Sir. But it is a calculated risk that I have decided to take."

"Ok. But we do not want you to leave. You have a bright future ahead in the bank and I hope you will give it another thought. Do you want an increase in your pay?"

"No, Sir."

"Do you want a higher grade?"

"No Sir, I am happy with whatever the bank has given me so far, without even asking."

"Ok, let us not hurry this. We are not accepting your resignation right now. I assure you that the bank will give you whatever you want. Let us talk this over next week."

He disconnected the telephone before I could say anything. I could sense his unhappiness. It was an emotional moment for me to think that my bosses were concerned about me quitting the bank. For a fraction of a second, I wondered if I should reconsider my decision and look beyond and not allow myself to be simply locked into what I had created. However, I brushed aside that thought.

Meanwhile, I continued with my work as usual. Since I was also filling in for the Regional Manager who was on leave, I had to put in long hours at the office to complete things on time. I prided myself on not keeping anything pending.

Mr Langer's words, "It is not a great idea to start a joint venture in which you have zero experience," kept bothering me for several days. Was I overlooking the potential to understand what will or will not happen once I quit my job? Was I being impulsive? Was I ignoring any signals being sent my way? I had only questions that I was asking myself, no clear answers.

CHAPTER FORTY-NINE

In the meantime, work continued as usual in the bank. I received a proposal for loan approval from one of the branches I was managing. It was the first one I picked up in the morning. I went through the customer file. Since we were not fully computerized, we had to rely on manual records available at the branch. I was alarmed by the fact that the branch, at least on four previous occasions (before my taking over) had recommended a sanction of a fresh loan, even though the previous loan was still outstanding.

I figured that the outstanding balance was then paid off from the new loan that was sanctioned, even though this practice was prohibited per the terms of the loans. The customer was supposed to pay off the loans using their funds and not by borrowing more from the bank. I also found irregularities in the payment of the loan and interest instalment. Even though there was no serious default, I was suspicious of the transactions.

I decided to investigate the matter, as it was a personal loan with no collateral and only a personal guarantee. I decided to visit the branch and talk to the manager to make sure there was no nexus between the branch manager and the customer.

Knowing that branch manager Mr Mansour was not fluent in English, I decided to take the assistance of Mr Ashraf Aziz, whom I knew at the branch I had started.

I called Mr Mansour to inform him that I would visit the branch the next day, I asked him to make sure that no staff would leave the branch until I met them. His assistant called me to find out the reason for my sudden visit. I did not give him any details and asked them to wait. As I had intended, my instructions created a highly speculative atmosphere.

I called Mr Aziz and requested him to accompany me the next day to the branch without giving him the reason or purpose of my visit. He was reluctant initially as it was also the holy month of Ramadan when Muslims fast from sunrise to sunset. I assured him that we would be back before Iftar (the time when the fast is broken). He agreed. The branch was an hour and a half away. On the way, I explained the purpose of my visit to Mr Aziz. I requested him to translate to Mr Mansour exactly what I said, and also to tell me exactly word by word what he said in response. I gathered that Mr Aziz was not aware of my resignation.

When we reached the branch, Mr Mansour greeted us courteously. The branch had only one closed-door cabin, occupied by the branch manager. Generally, whenever I visited any branch I would always occupy the guest chair even if offered by the manager to occupy theirs. I politely requested Mr Mansour to allow me and Mr Aziz to occupy his cabin for some time. Instantly and without any hesitancy he agreed and walked out.

I started calling the branch staff one by one asking them about the working of the branch, what their job description was, and other such questions without giving anyone the slightest hint of the purpose of my visit. I called a key credit department employee, let's call him Yasser. I found him to be smart. After a few formal questions, I asked him the same set of questions that I had asked the others including 'Who are the top five customers of the branch?' He named them and it tallied with my list. However, this list did not include the name of the customer about whom I wanted to inquire. Now, relaxed I asked him, "Can you tell me about Mr Yousuf, the client? How is he?" Yasser responded "He is a nice person. He is a friend of the manager."

This intrigued me. I pointedly asked him what the relationship between the manager and Mr Yousuf was outside of banking. Yasser said, "Mr Yousuf invited the branch manager to go along with his family to Europe on a fully-paid vacation – twice."

I asked Yasser to leave.

I got what I wanted. Mr Aziz said, "Vijay, your doubt is confirmed."

I called the rest of the staff. When finished, I went out of the cabin and announced that everyone could leave now if they wanted to.

I invited Mr Mansour to join me and Mr Aziz. I got up from his chair and invited him to sit in his chair. Mr Aziz and I occupied the guest chairs.

I asked him, "Mr Mansour, this is the holy month of Ramadan. I expect you to tell me the truth."

He said, "Sure Sir, I will."

"Mr Mansour, how is your client, Mr Yousuf?"

"He is good and reputed in the business circle here."

"Does he have a company borrowing account with us or only a personal loan?"

"Only a personal loan account with us. His company account is with another bank."

"Why are you not trying to get his company account?"

"Mr Vijay, I have been trying for a few years now. He has promised to do so shortly."

"Good, how reliable is he?"

"Very much. I can vouch for him. He is a good person."

"Have you tried to get a balance sheet of his company?"

"No, I have not. I will make sure that I get it shortly."

"Okay, when you get that, please send me a copy."

"Sure Sir."

I went on to probe, "Does he have a clean image in the market?"

"Yes Sir."

"How are you so sure about it?"

"I have asked a couple of our customers who are in the same business."

"Good. What are your relations with him? Beyond banking?"

"I have good personal relations with him."

"How good? Have you exchanged family visits?"

"Yes."

"How often?"

"At least once a month."

"Have you been frequently going with him on any pleasure tours within and outside UAE?"

"No Sir."

"So you have full trust in him?"

"Yes."

"Is that why you have been recommending a fresh loan for him frequently even before his old loan is fully paid off? And his outstanding loan is made good from the new loan?"

"Yes Sir."

"Have you ever tried to obtain any collateral for his loan? Or at least asked him to place some amount in a fixed deposit?"

"No, Sir I have not."

"Why not?"

"Because he enjoys a good market reputation and I want to get his company account."

"You said that you have not seen his company's balance sheet, how are you so sure about his company's financials that you are chasing him to open his company account with us?"

"He has told me about his turnover and profits – but I will ask him to give me the company balance sheet in a day or two."

"Are you sure he will give it to you?"

"Yes Sir, if I ask him for it, and he will give it to me."

"Don't forget to send me a copy."

"I will do that."

"Mr Mansour, let me ask you candidly. How much has he personally favoured you that has prompted you to recommend a new loan without his paying off his old loan from his resources?"

"Mr Vijay, why are you asking this?"

In a stern tone, I responded, "How much has he has favoured you to do this directly or indirectly?"

"No, nothing Sir."

"Would you be happy if I sanction a higher loan amount than you have sought?"

"That will be great."

"I may do that, but first tell me how much he has favoured you, directly or indirectly."

"Nothing, Sir."

"Come clean on this Mr Mansour. Please tell me the truth."

"I am telling you the truth."

"No, you are not."

"I swear, I am."

"Did he take you and your family on any overseas tour?"

"No, that is a lie."

"On a European tour?"

"No."

"Are you sure? Not once, but twice?"

"That is not correct. Who told you this?"

"Don't bother about that Mr Mansour. Just tell me the truth and you will not lose your job."

He hesitated.

"I am telling you the truth."

"One last time Mr Mansour. I have my sources to find out even on what exact dates you have travelled with him with your families. Please remember that if I do that you will lose your job."

He broke down.

"Yes Sir. He took me and my family to Europe twice at his expense."

"And how much direct monetary favour? 5%?" It was a shot in the dark.

"No, not 5%, 3%."

"At least finally you have told me the truth."

"Sir, I plead with you to save my job. I am a Palestinian, and I have five children. We do not have a homeland, where will I go? Please save my job!"

"I am glad that you have now come clean. Now tell me in the name of God that you will never indulge in such acts, wherever and whichever position you are in. Ever."

"In the name of God, I swear."

"Okay, then I promise you that I will try my best to see that you will not lose your bank job. Mr Mansour, please always remember, if facts make you uncomfortable and nervous, you must resolve not to be in this kind of a situation again, for the sake of yourself and your family. Good Day."

I left with Mr Aziz. On the way, he told me, "Vijay, you are tough but kind. Will you always remain my friend? I said sure Mr Aziz, it is my honour to be your friend." He took my hand in his. I could feel the warmth in it.

CHAPTER FIFTY

After a quick lunch at home, I went back to the office. I requested Flavia to come after dinner and bring her husband along as it might get late by the time we finished. I also informed the bank's driver to be ready to travel the next day to the Head Office around 5:30 a.m. to ensure that the packets reached Mr Lewis and Mr Langer before 8 a.m. when banking hours started.

I prepared a detailed report on my visit to the branch, describing my conversation with the manager Mr Mansour, my findings and recommendations. Flavia arrived with her husband. This was the first time I was asking her to come to the bank at night and she and her husband were puzzled. I apologised for inconveniencing her. I explained the document and what and how I wanted it to be typed. While she was typing I engaged her husband in conversation as we were meeting after a long time. I guessed he knew that I had resigned.

She finished her job, made whatever changes and corrections I wanted, made two packets, one marked to Michael Lewis and the other to Dan Langer. I carried both the packets home for the driver to collect from my residence early the next day, which he did.

I found the manager guilty of taking and giving undue favours to the customer and established that his act was unethical. I recommended that he be demoted by two grades and be transferred to a non-operational related department such as the mail section.

It was Dan Langer who called me first.

"Good morning Vijay. Have you decided to withdraw your resignation?"

"No Sir."

"Then why did you take the trouble of going to the branch? I went through the report, and I appreciate it. However, if you are not going to withdraw your resignation you could have just sent me a note to set up an inquiry against Mansour. I would have done the needful."

"Sir, I will be paid my salary until the last day of my work. So it is my responsibility to complete it and not keep anything pending against my name when I leave."

"Yeah, Vijay. You will never change. Okay, look I went through your findings on Mansour. It is a pretty detailed description and I do not have any counter questions. But I do not agree with your recommendation on punishments to be awarded to Mansour."

"Any particular reason, Sir? Is it too harsh?"

"No, it is not harsh. He needs to be sacked, nothing less. And why do you want to be so lenient with him?"

"Sir, mainly for two reasons. One, there is no financial loss to the bank. Two, on humanitarian grounds. I promised him if he comes clean and tells me the truth he will not lose his job. Sir, he has responsibilities towards his wife and five children."

"I am not convinced."

"Sir, I understand. But I still request you to please accept my recommendations."

"Just because you have promised him?"

"Sir, if you feel that I have always performed my duties in the best interest of the bank, please consider my request. When you received my resignation you told me that you will give me whatever I want. I will never forget your gesture. I want only one thing from the bank. Please do not sack Mr Mansour as I have promised him. I will take this as a personal obligation to me."

"Well, let me think. I will come back to you tomorrow."

"Thank you, Sir. I will wait for your decision."

Mr Lewis called me a short while later. We had an almost identical conversation. Somehow I was confident that the management would agree with my recommendation.

The next day, Mr Langer again called me.

"Vijay, yesterday, the CEO Jim Chambers, Michael Lewis and I met and discussed your findings in detail.

Jim was in favour of sacking him. I gave them a detailed account of our telephone conversation. Jim asked me for my opinion. I told him that I will go with Vijay's recommendations. He looked at Michael, who was also in agreement with me. Jim then said, 'Do it for Vijay. Make him happy.' Are you happy now?"

"Thank you very much, Sir."

He went on, "Jim wants to talk to you. Can you call him now?"

"Yes Sir. I will call him right away."

I immediately called him.

"Good morning Sir, this is Vijay."

"Good morning Vijay. So what have you decided about your resignation?"

"Sir, I am firm."

"Dan Langer has conveyed this to you, and I again wanted to reiterate – if you want anything from the bank, let us know and we will take care of that. You are set to conquer new heights in the bank."

"Thank you Sir for your generous offer and very kind gesture. But as of now, I do not think I will change my decision."

"Michael and Dan have given me the details behind your resignation. If there is anything in the future come back to us."

"Thank you, Sir."

I called Mr Langer and briefed him about my conversation with the CEO.

I asked him, "So when are you accepting my resignation? I am awaiting your acceptance."

He responded, "I am yet to make up my mind, but take two days to think through it and then call me with your final decision."

"I will do that Sir."

Meanwhile, Mr Lewis tried to convince me to withdraw my resignation. After two days I called Mr Langer and informed him that I was not changing my decision.

He finally said, "Vijay, you are not leaving any option for me but to accept your resignation. I do so with a heavy heart. Tomorrow, you will get a formal acceptance letter from HR."

"Thank you, Sir."

I became emotional.

I realized my true value in the bank. I do realize that it appeared to be at the risk of my image being perceived as a perfect being.

CHAPTER FIFTY-ONE

The next day I received the letter accepting my resignation. At the same time, a telex came from HR, copied to all the banks, domestic and overseas and overseas correspondents worldwide.

It read:

Mr Vijay Thariani has resigned from the services of the bank. Consequently, with immediate effect, his discretionary powers stand withdrawn.

I called Mr Lewis and informed him about the telex. I asked who was going to approve the new loans and other credit proposals since the Regional Manager was on leave.

He told me to give him a few minutes. "I will talk to Dan Langer and come back to you." After approximately five minutes, he called me again inquiring where the telex had come from. I informed him that it had come from HR and that I thought it was a normal practice. He asked me to wait for the next telex from HR.

After approximately ten minutes, there was a second telex from HR copied to all recipients of their previous telex. The latest one read: *Our previous telex concerning the discretionary powers of Mr Vijay Thariani stands cancelled.*

His discretionary and signature powers shall remain in force till his last day at work, September 30.

Flavia, who brought the telex to me was still in my office. She perhaps saw my misty eyes.

She said, "Sir, congratulations. I have been in our bank for 15 years, but I have never seen anything like this. Your resignation was accepted but all your financial and administrative powers remain until the last day of work." Her voice was choked with emotion. I thanked her and requested her to connect me to Mr Lewis in a while. However, after 10 minutes, I called for tea, recouped myself and instead of asking Flavia to connect me to Mr Lewis, I called him from my direct line.

I began, "Sir, thank you very much for your confidence in me. I am honoured."

"Not at all. Vijay. We trust your prudence. I was wondering why HR was in a rush to send the telexes without even talking to me or Dan or Jim."

"Sir, in most banks this is the normal practice. Have you decided on my replacement? I now have only three weeks before I leave."

He asked, "Whom do you recommend?"

I gave him three names. He was not impressed with any.

He ended the call saying, "We will inform you in due course."

With telexes going to multiple branches, all the branch managers and their credit team started calling me to find out why and wishing me good luck for the future. Just as I was replying and thanking everyone, Mr Mansour called me to say, "Mr Vijay, Thank you very much. I just received a memo from Head Office that I have been transferred to the mail section of Abu Dhabi Main Branch." Maybe he wanted to say more but could not because of the limitations of his English vocabulary. He said, "Best of luck." I could hear his deep breaths over the phone. I said, "I hope you will keep your promise to me." He said, "Sure, I promise you again."

In the following days, I made sure that no work remained pending for the next day. Mr Lewis would call me at least once a day, discuss some customer accounts, and invariably touch the subject of my resignation or ask me my opinion on a certain name as my replacement.

One day he told me, "Vijay, why don't you assess all the credit personnel of your region?" I assured him that I would do so within the next 24 hours. I made a chart and against each name, I scored them on a scale of 10. The highest I could go was only 7, but against one name, Hamid Taylor, my remarks were, "It is difficult for me to judge Mr Hamid Taylor on a scale of 10. I am not adequately qualified to do that. Still, I give him 10 on 10 with a request that he be accommodated at the head office as he can easily walk into the shoes of any executive position in the bank." I sent the report.

As expected I received a call from Mr Lewis the next morning.

"Vijay, why have you not included your Regional Manager?"

"Sir, I cannot. It will not be correct to give my opinion on my direct boss."

"That is fine. I want you to do that and send me the reviewed list. It will be the basis of deciding your replacement. And, I know Hamid Taylor is your close friend, but don't you think you are being generous in your appraisal of him? I am sure even Dan Langer and Jim Chambers would not compliment me the way you have complimented Hamid."

"Sir, I cannot comment on it. However, I have been honest in my assessment without considering my friendship with Mr Taylor. Having worked closely with him, I have no hesitation in saying that I consider him to be a complete banker. I have learned a lot from him. In addition to him being professional while discharging his duties, he is also a noble individual. A fine human being. I feel that it is a rare combination. I am also of the firm opinion that Hamid Taylor's talent and capabilities are being wasted here in Dubai. I strongly recommend absorbing him in decision-making teams at the head office."

"OK, I will keep that in mind." Mr Lewis said before signing off.

Meanwhile, I kept getting copied on memos exchanged among Jim Chambers, Michael Lewis and Dan Langer about my replacement. They could not decide on any one individual. I would not comment, respond or even try to participate in their discussion, except once when Hamid Taylor's name appeared. I wrote back. "This position is too insignificant for Hamid Taylor."

After this exchange, the last memo on the subject that I received was signed by Michael Lewis and endorsed by Jim Chambers and Dan Langer. It read, "I cannot find a suitable replacement for Mr Vijay. I recommend that we advertise the vacancy for the position and recruit preferably a British or American national." The next day, the same memo was repeated but the last four words – "British or American national – were deleted." It proved that appropriate protocols should be honoured for both visible and invisible affinities.

CHAPTER FIFTY-TWO

I could not find words to express my feelings. For the first time, I had realized my value in the bank. If I have to describe it I would say it was an "out of the world" experience. I had seen a few resignations during my tenure with the bank for some key positions. And to the best of my knowledge, senior management may have asked them if there was a particular reason for their resignation. I had not heard of any persuasion which made my experience more special. The Regional Manager returned from his leave just a few days before my last day of work. He was extremely surprised and shocked when he learnt of my resignation.

He introduced an angle beyond the persuasion method that had been used thus far. He said that he will allow me to take a no-pay leave for as long as I liked – up to six months. I politely declined, but I did think that if I was offered this option earlier, perhaps I may have accepted it.

I asked him for a replacement and also asked Flavia to place all the memos on my resignation, on his desk. He spoke with Mr Lewis and Mr Langer. After speaking to them he asked me to call Mr Langer.

I called.

"Sir, good morning. There is just one day left. To whom should I hand over the charge? I asked the Regional Manager. He asked me to check with you. Today is Wednesday and tomorrow is my last working day. Friday is a holiday. My resignation is effective from Saturday. Should I leave the keys with him or do you have someone in mind who would call me later in the day?"

"Vijay…"

"Yes, Sir."

"Take the keys home on Thursday. Reconsider your decision. On Saturday, go to the office. If you decide to change your decision, just pick up the phone and let me know. I will do what is required. If not, leave keys with the Regional Manager. I will tell him what to do."

"Yes, Sir, I will do that."

I felt blessed. Honoured.

After my lunch on Thursday, I went back to the office in the evening to make sure that I did not have any pending work. There was none.

I prepared a detailed transition plan for my successor with a ready reference for the credit staff of all branches. In addition to a complete job description of what I was doing, I also documented the regional budget, monthly visits to the Northern Region branches, top five clients of each branch and status of the accounts.

I came home with mixed feelings and my mood swung between relaxed and stressed. Jaya and I could not sleep the whole night pondering over our decision and whether we should reconsider or not.

The next day, a Friday, Mr Lewis called me around noon and tried to persuade me again to withdraw my resignation. Perhaps my destiny did not allow me to reconsider and respond positively to such rare gestures that were being shown by my management team. I had never seen, heard or read about any such measures ever taken by my management.

On Saturday, I went to the office at my scheduled time. The staff speculated and wondered if I would continue. Everyone asked me and I just smiled. The Regional Manager had not come in as yet and I called Mr Langer.

"Good morning, Sir."

"Good morning, Vijay. I am in a mood to hear some good news from you."

"My apologies to you, Sir, but I am not changing my decision."

"That is unfortunate. Please hand over your keys to the Regional Manager. And by the way, I am informing you that as of now, we have not finalized anyone to replace you. I wish you all the very best."

"Thank you very much, Sir."

For a few moments, I was lost in thought.

When the Regional Manager came to the office, I informed him of my decision and my conversation with Mr Langer. I thanked him for his support and apologized for not changing my mind. He wished me a bright, new career and as he held my hand, he shook it warmly and said, "I hope that one day you decide to re-join us."

At that point, I also had another option given to me by the Regional Manager – withdraw my resignation, take six months' unpaid leave, then take a final call.

However, destiny had already written my future. I was helpless. But was I?

A warm farewell was organized at the Regional Office. It was well attended by most Regional Officers and I received phone calls wishing me all the best from everyone with whom I had associated at any point in the bank.

The CEO Mr Chambers, Mr Lewis and HR heads also called me as did Mr Mansour. I was pleasantly surprised to get a call from Mr Adil Rahman, my erstwhile colleague and the then Director-General, Dubai Chamber of Commerce, bidding me farewell and issuing me an open invitation to meet him when I visited the UAE next. I did not know who had informed him about my going back to India for good.

Several thoughts crossed my mind including, "Is it worth quitting when you are at the top?" Only the future would answer this. Isn't it strange that we are unable to see our future, yet we attempt to shape the present in such a way as to protect it?

CHAPTER FIFTY-THREE

Jaya and I left the UAE for good. It was a working day. Hamidbhai and Najmabhabhi had come to the airport to see us off. We arrived in India. My parents were not happy that I had quit a steady job overseas and come back to India against their wishes.

I do not blame them. Our family has a history of being working professionals. My father, brother, sisters were all working professionals. I took their disappointment in my stride. Instead of taking it to heart, I concentrated on beginning the new phase of my life. Our household goods that were shipped from the UAE were received and arranged in the house making it feel like a home.

The new shop was in the final stages of furnishing. I would visit the market to familiarize myself with the business. Let me admit that things did not appear to be as rosy as I had thought. Deep down I was concerned about not being able to settle in the business and I spent many sleepless nights worrying about the consequences. Finally, I accepted the fact that I will be where destiny wants me to be. This acceptance helped me gather a good amount of confidence.

Before the opening of the shop, I became friendly with two gentlemen who were traders cum brokers –

Jethabhai and Prembhai. They were supportive, always encouraging me, assuring me that they would extend their expertise and experience as and when needed. That made me feel better and added to my confidence.

The opening day arrived. Several clients, traders, brokers, relatives, friends and family were invited to join the celebration.

As I interacted with the people, I sensed that I was in a group of people different from the ones I had been interacting with just a few months ago. However, I told myself that it was too early for me to judge anyone and I managed to continue. I could not deny the fact that I had made my choice and I did not allow my enthusiasm to falter.

Every guest was at first surprised at my background and then impressed. It was not hard to imagine that things would change and would never be the same as in Dubai, but I told myself to accept reality.

On the way home, Jaya asked me, "Are you okay?" I told her, "I am fine but I feel a bit tired." I was thinking of the day when *Dada* told me he was in a partnership and he and his partners had a difference of opinion. I was only 22 years old when he told me his story. He shared the difficulties he faced in the business with his partners. He had a partnership agreement where he owned 25% of the business. He told me that he had been advised by some of his close relatives and friends as well as market traders to bring an injunction on the business, have the business premises sealed and force his partners to settle his account. He told me that he was in favour of going ahead with initiating legal action.

I was young at the time and a working professional in a bank. I did not know the nuances of the business world. However, I told him that I did not think it was advisable to take legal action. I told him that I believed that legal action would only increase the bitterness. I used an analogy. "Suppose you are sitting under a tree resting and there is a strong wind that blows and a fruit falls on your head. Does it mean that you will uproot the tree?"

Days, weeks and months passed. I learnt the essence of the business. I built excellent relationships with our suppliers, brokers, and customers. I felt that I had travelled a long way over the last several months – from not knowing the business to getting a good grip and learning the tricks of the trade.

CHAPTER FIFTY-FOUR

We were nearing the close of our working day. A man with his wife and kids entered the shop. He gave me the name of a shop and asked if this was the shop that had been recommended to him. It turned out that the first name was the same but the second name was different.

I told him, "No, the shop you are looking for is in the other lane," and I gave him directions to go there. He asked if we dealt in yellow sapphires. Yellow Sapphires are considered lucky stones and signify success and prosperity. I told him that we did deal in them. He asked if he could see some. I said yes, but that he should please first go to the shop that was recommended to him. I let him know that if he did not get what he wanted, he could come back to me and I could help him out.

As soon as the family left, some of the traders including Jethabhai and Prembhai as well as my partners were surprised and disbelieving. All of them were unanimous in telling me, "How could you allow a customer to go?"

I told them, "In my opinion, even if I would have tried to force the sale, he was sure to visit the other shop. I thought that it was better if he first visited them and then came back rather than the other way around." All of them were sure that the customer would not come back. I kept calm.

Within the next ten minutes, the same family came back and asked to see yellow sapphires. I asked, "Did you not get anything from there?" The man answered in the negative. I showed them several varieties of yellow sapphires and I was able to make a sale of an expensive stone.

As a matter of policy I offered him a trial of seven days, within which if he got any negative vibes from the stone, he could return the same stone for a full refund.

He said, "Thanks, but no." He said he wanted to buy the stone and asked if we could make him a ring. He also asked, "Can you please send it home?" I agreed, but told him, "Once you make the ring and if you want to return the stone, our terms will be different. You will not get a full refund." He said that he was fine with it.

As we were completing the paperwork, he was sipping orange juice and singing in a low voice. I thought he had a good voice. I asked him his name, "KS," he replied.

He was an upcoming Bollywood singer and had sung for many movies. A recent movie that he had sung for had become popular upon its release. I looked at him and smiled and everyone else in the shop got up to shake hands with him. Nobody had left for the day, even though it was well beyond closing hours.

Before leaving, he asked me, "Do you know why I came back so fast after you directed me to the shop I asked for?" I said, "I think you told me that you did not get anything from there to your satisfaction." He said, "As a matter of fact I went, glanced at the shop and came back. Before I landed up at your shop, I went to a couple of other shops in the same street. No one gave me directions to the shop I was asking, instead, they were trying to force me to see their stock. You were the only one different from them. I appreciated your honesty and that is the real reason I came back."

"Thank you," I said.

Mr KS went on to win many reputed singing awards and on his fingers were rings embedded with lucky stones – all supplied by us.

The people in the shop listened to this conversation in disbelief. Jethabhai and Prembhai said, "Today we have learned a lesson."

News of this particular incident spread in the market and the attitude of many traders and suppliers noticeably changed towards me. I started commanding more respect.

However, I still was not comfortable with the new setup. I had to focus on not getting consumed by my negative state of mind.

Jethabhai and Prembhai on several occasions tried to find the truth as to why I always look stressed out and not in the best of moods. Though we were close friends, I did not share anything with them.

Stress often destabilizes the mind dramatically. It gives birth to internal unrest if it is allowed to be prolonged. It can adversely affect social equilibrium. The last thing that anyone needs in life is a complex conflict within oneself. It is a red flag and a roadblock in the way of a smooth and peaceful life. One can easily end up fighting a losing battle on most of life's fronts.

Fortunately, I never had to pay a price for my promise to Jaya that I would never mix family relationships and business matters. On the contrary, I was rewarded with mental stability and peace. It proved to be my most powerful weapon to enable me to sail through a rather unpleasant phase of my life.

CHAPTER FIFTY-FIVE

During my work, I was fortunate to come into contact with another trader, Pratapbhai and we soon became friends. As I got to know him, I started respecting him for his transparency and straightforwardness. We shared the same respect amongst others in the market and soon became members of a mutual admiration club.

Pratapbhai would often call me during business hours to exchange views on a wide range of subjects – be it business, India's economy, politics, spiritual, religious, or human relationships. Our conversations would often involve a recurring theme of honesty and we would ask ourselves – could no business be done with honesty and integrity? We would only agree on the question but alas could not see evidence of the right answer being practised.

I also want to make a specific mention of another market friend, Sunilbhai Parikh. His father had long-standing business relations with our firm for several years. When Sunilbhai was first introduced to us by his father, I found him to be a straightforward person.

Over time as I became close to him, we would share many things. I found him to be honest in business deals. He also acted as a broker and I always trusted him to close a business deal, on our behalf, as he felt appropriate. Without exception, he always was able to do so, well below our suggested price. Besides a business relationship, we also became friends.

One day, I was pleasantly surprised to get a call from Hambidbhai letting me know that he was in Bombay. We met after about a year. We shared our stories and I was happy to learn that after I had left the bank, he was transferred to the head office and was rewarded with three promotions in a little over six months.

While we were talking, I asked him if it would be possible for me to get back to the bank. He was smart enough to guess that I was not happy with my business set-up. He said that he would go back and let me know.

He called me after about three months to let me know that the CEO and Regional Manager were coming to Bombay. He asked if I could meet them and that he had spoken to them about me. He gave me their schedule in Bombay. I called them at the appointed date and time. After greeting me, they immediately asked when I would be able to join the bank.

I looked at them and asked them to give me two to three months. Both agreed and asked me to inform Hamid Taylor of the decision/timing. I immediately called Hamidbhai on the phone and he was happy to hear the news.

I informed Jaya of my meetings with the CEO and Regional Manager, and Hamidbhai's contribution to it. Hamidbhai and I exchanged many calls during working hours and therefore my business associates got a sense of what I intended to do. I was all set to go back to UAE – only the date was to be decided.

At this time, Jaya's younger brother, Jaggi, fell ill. It was unexpected. He was admitted to the hospital. He slipped into a coma and was diagnosed with a stage 3 malignant brain tumour. He was operated upon in an emergency but unfortunately could not recover. He headed for his heavenly journey within five days of being admitted to the hospital, leaving us all in deep grief.

After his 12th and 13th day rituals, Jaya's mother talked to her. She told Jaya that she heard through her children that Vijabhai and Hamidbhai were in constant touch and that we were planning to go back to Dubai.

She pleaded with Jaya not to go back saying that they would be alone without us. She cried a lot. Jaya too was upset seeing her mother sobbing. I had already started deliberating on what we should do under the circumstances.

I know that my partners had bought a bigger shop because I had consented to join them. I wondered whether they would have waited to make this investment if they knew I would return to Dubai. I was in a dilemma –

should we stick to the decision to head back or decide otherwise?

If I decided to go back, I would leave them with two hands short in the business. Another option we explored was that I would go back alone while Jaya and the children would stay back in Bombay for the time being. Would it be proper for me to do so? It was a real dilemma. But we needed to come to a decision.

Should we be selfish but practical about our future? Or, should we continue with the current situation which would give us self-satisfaction that we did not desert our family in their difficult time?

After a lot of deliberation, Jaya and I took a joint decision. We decided that we did not want to do something where our conscience bites us. We dropped our plans to return to Dubai, thereby not deserting our family in times of need.

I called Hamidbhai and explained everything to him. I told him that my conscience was not permitting me to leave Bombay. He knew the circumstances and details when I left UAE to join the business and said, "Vijay, I fully understand. Do what your conscience says. Not many in a similar situation as you and *Bhabhi* would take such a decision."

Jaya and I were at peace and we derived immense satisfaction after deciding to stay back.

CHAPTER FIFTY-SIX

Meanwhile, I acquired a sub-broker ship with a broker of the Bombay Stock Exchange. Jaya called my attention to an advertisement published in a newspaper. The Pune Stock Exchange was inviting membership applications. I applied, appeared in a written test, interviewed, and was selected.

I would have to visit Pune frequently. I wondered if it could be possible to leave the business and rely only on the Pune Stock Exchange (PSE) for my income. Then again, if I did that, my purpose of not going back to the UAE would be defeated.

Would it be fair, if I continued in the business while frequently travelling to Pune? Would it be fair even if my other partners did not mind it? My conscience said no again. So, I offered my partners a partnership in the stock brokerage business. They agreed. I also briefed my nephew, Prakash, who happened to be the co-brother of Abu, my brother-in-law and partner. He agreed. Prakash has always been like a younger brother to me and is my confidant. We signed partnership agreements after agreeing to all the terms.

We hired an experienced person to handle our day-to-day brokerage activity in Pune. I would go every week to check the books and make sure everything was working well. Occasionally, Prakash or one of my other partners would go to Pune.

Our business was increasing and we needed to hire additional staff. We advertised in the local newspapers and received 10 applications.

My daughter Rachana and I went to Pune for the interviews. Rachana had already completed her B.Com and was looking after my sub-brokership business in Bombay, prior to my acquiring membership of Pune Stock Exchange.

We began the selection process by interviewing candidates. She did most of the talking and noted down her assessment of each candidate. One person who came for the interview was a young girl, Shalini Mascarenhas. We found her perfect for the job as she was already working with another stockbroker of Pune Stock Exchange.

Rachana asked about her salary expectations. She said her current salary was Rs. 1,200 but she was willing to work at even a lower salary. We asked her why that was the case. Hesitatingly, she said that her employer was not a good man and she was desperate to find a new job. Her mother was a nurse and father was a small-time mechanic. Her brother was still studying.

Rachana asked her to wait. We interviewed other candidates but found Shalini to be the most suitable.

Rachana and I decided that if she accepted our offer, we should drive over to her parents' place to meet them so that they know who their daughter would be working for.

Rachana said, "Pappa, she is willing to work for 1200 rupees or less, but a significant portion of her salary will go towards transport. Looking at her experience and intelligence we should at least give her 50% more than what she is getting now. Remember also to give her regular increments if she turns out to be good and competent."

I immediately agreed and told her to decide the salary. I felt proud to be a father of a kind-hearted and intelligent daughter.

We called Shalini in and informed her that we were selecting her for the job. We then told her that we would like to visit her home and meet her parents so that they knew (and felt good about) her new job. We asked when we could visit her home. She said that we could go immediately if we wanted to. She said that her parents would be waiting for her to reach home to find out about the job interview. She did not ask about salary – not even a hint of a question.

Rachana asked her, "Do you not want to ask how much we will pay you?"

She said, "Ma'am you have appointed me that is more than enough for me."

We could sense her desperate need to quit her current job at the earliest opportunity.

Rachana went on, "What if we offer you less than what you are drawing now?"

"I will accept it."

"And if we tell you that we will match your current salary?"

"I will be happy".

"Now, let us know at what salary you will be very happy?"

"Rs. 1200 will make me very happy."

"How much are you spending on transport?"

"Nearly Rs. 500 per month. I have to change buses."

"Okay, please sit outside. We will call you again."

Rachana asked me what I thought. I asked her to make a decision and whatever she decided was fine by me.

Shalini was called in again.

Rachana said, "Look Shalini, after considering everything we are offering you Rs. 1800 per month, subject to your parents agreeing on you working for us."

"How much?" Shalini asked in surprise.

"Rs. 1800," Rachana repeated.

Shalini said, "I never even dreamt of this figure. I can't believe it…"

Rachana clarified, "Shalini, we have considered everything. Your experience, your need, transportation expenses, etc. We feel that we are reasonable and not being unnecessarily generous."

With tears of joy rolling down her eyes, Shalini said, "Thank you very much, madam."

We drove to her house. Her parents were happy to see their daughter's bosses coming personally to meet them to seek their permission. They agreed and expressed their gratitude. We gave them our Bombay numbers if they needed anything from us. We asked Shalini to join work the day after her last working day with her current employer. Rachana and I were perhaps more satisfied with our decision than ever before. I looked at Rachana. She said, "Pappa, it is good we hired her."

Rachana's assessment of Shalini was 100% correct. Until I decided to call it a day with the Pune Stock Exchange, Shalini was employed with us. She was drawing a salary of Rs. 6,000 by then and provided her with a company two-wheeler. When we closed the business, we gave her the two-wheeler – not at its depreciated value but as a token of our appreciation for her hard work over so many years.

CHAPTER FIFTY-SEVEN

As I said earlier, Rachana was managing our brokerage business in Bombay after completing her B.Com. She and Jaya were in favour of her pursuing a post-graduation program. I was not in favour and felt that if she did her post-graduation, it would be difficult for us to find a suitable match for her from our community. Jaya was not happy and disagreed with my views.

She kept inquiring with Rachana's friends when they visited our house, about post-graduation courses and the career opportunities they presented.

One day, we went to see a doctor as I had discomfort in my chest. While we were waiting for my turn, Jaya came across an article on the industrialist, Kumar Mangalam Birla (KMB), from the famous Birla family.

As we were returning from the check-up, Jaya shared the details of KMB's education and his background. She said, "Look, KMB is born in a rich industrialist family. He is the heir apparent of a business empire. Why was he not inducted into the family business right away after his graduation? Why did he opt to do an MBA?"

She continued, "There must be something about higher education that he and his parents thought was important. And we are waiting for her match. We have received so many proposals for her but we are not satisfied with any of them. I think we must allow her to study further. Leave the rest to destiny."

I agreed instantly. We informed Rachana. She jumped at our proposal and started preparing for the MBA program. After this, I became a staunch supporter of the MBA program and the shell of my shallow thinking was broken.

CHAPTER FIFTY-EIGHT

Meanwhile, my weekly trips to Pune continued. One day, one of my trader friends expressed his desire to join me with his family, to inquire about schools with hostel facilities in Pune for his children.

We planned to travel to Pune on March 1, 1997. The entire state was plunged into darkness a day earlier because the power grid had tripped. My father had been hospitalized during that time and he was discharged late in the evening at around 8 p.m. when the power was restored.

Around midnight, my father woke me up and asked, "Vijay, what if you don't go to Pune tomorrow?"

I thought that he was perhaps nervous as he had come home after spending a week in the hospital. I told him that I had to go. He asked me to take care and to only go if I had to.

I reassured him that I was not going alone - my friend and his family were also travelling with me. He did not say anything and went back to sleep. At approximately 6 a.m. the next morning, we started for Pune in my Maruti 800.

Since I was a regular traveller, I was familiar with the road conditions. These were the days before the expressway and the travel to Pune was largely on a single road.

My normal driving routine was such that when I started from Bombay, I would switch on the air conditioner and switch it off before arriving at Khandala Ghat so that the car would not overheat. After crossing the Lonavala bus depot, I would switch it on again. It was a weekly routine. On that day, as my friend and I were busy talking, I saw Kamshet Ghat in the distance, six kilometres after crossing the depot. I realized that I had not switched on the air conditioner again.

I told my friend and his family that I was doing so. Before I could complete my sentence, the car suddenly overturned, its wheels up in the air and sliding along on its roof. I did not know what happened. We were upside down. When the car stopped sliding, we found ourselves standing on the road with the doors completely smashed. The car had slid from the Bombay-to-Pune side to the Pune-to-Bombay side of the road.

While the car was sliding, Mataji's small *chunni* (scarf) was touching my head. The Vaishnodevi temple is in Pimpri, a suburb of Pune. The scarf was changed on every trip to Pune and was always tied to the rear-view mirror. I distinctly remember that I remained calm. I did not panic and the first thought that crossed my mind as the car slid on its roof was that nothing would happen to me.

As we were standing by the side of the road, I was numb and was unable to think of what to do next. My friend who was healthier and well-built was in the front seat while I was driving. His wife was bleeding a little from the nose. His three-year-old son had slight bleeding on the back of his neck but his daughters who were five and seven seemed safe.

I thanked God.

After a few minutes, I gathered my composure. Many cars stopped to ask us if we needed help. As soon as I was ready to seek help, I told my friend we needed first aid and some basic medical attention.

A mini-truck carrying sugarcane stopped and offered to take us to Lonavala where a hospital was authorized to treat accident cases even before the police arrived. We went with him.

I thought that someone had rear-ended us as there was no vehicle seen in front of me when the car overturned. We reached the hospital, underwent basic medical examination including x-rays.

Luckily, no one suffered any serious injuries. We had escaped with a few scratches. I suggested to my friend that he should go back to Bombay, undergo a detailed medical check-up and rule out any internal injuries. He agreed, hired a taxi and headed back to Bombay.

After he left I called Jaya and briefed her about the accident. I gave her the hospital address. She asked me to wait at the hospital and that they would start immediately.

In the meantime, four young boys came in their car and inquired about passengers involved in an accident. The hospital receptionist directed them to me. They told me that a truck had hit my car and that the driver and cleaner had fled. The boys managed to get the permit papers from the truck and handed them over to me. I quietly took the papers and thanked them. They said that they were headed to Bombay and asked if I needed any help or whether I needed to send a message to my family. I thanked them again and told them that I had already contacted my family and that they were on the way to see me.

A middle-aged man came and sat next to me. He asked me for details of the accident. He introduced himself as the Sarpanch (Chief) of Lonavala Gram Panchayat (Local Municipality). He offered me the hospitality of his home for rest and breakfast. I politely declined saying that I did not want to move from where I was. I did not want my family to panic when they arrived if they did not see me.

He understood and offered to send tea and snacks. He also informed me that it was the Gram Panchayat election day and the entire village police force would be busy. He told me that I would have to go to Vadgoan, approximately 18 km away from the hospital, if I wanted to file a complaint. I thanked him again. As promised, he sent tea and snacks.

After a couple of hours, Jaya, my sister-in-law Surekha, who is a doctor, my brothers-in-law Abu and Suresh, and my nephew Prakash arrived. They were tense but were relieved when they saw me. The knowledge that your family is always there for you in your tough times was very comforting.

Jaya, Surekha and I checked into a hotel. Abu, Suresh and Prakash went to the police station to file an FIR and complete police procedures. I gave them the bag containing the truck driver's permit and travel documents. After taking the medicines, I went off to sleep.

At around 2 p.m., Prakash called to inform me that they were bringing the Police Inspector to the hotel to record my statement. He told me that I would have to tell the police that a truck from the opposite side hit my car. Prakash said that the driver and cleaner of the truck were in the police station to collect their permit papers and that they had given a statement that the car driver ran into the truck from the opposite direction.

I said that was not true. I had not seen anything and I could not believe a truck was rushing in on my car from the opposite direction. Prakash told me that if I do not say what he asked me to say, the court will think that it was my fault and that I was inebriated while driving.

I told him I would not lie. He said that the inspector would write the statement and that I had to just sign the papers. I agreed but I was left wondering why the truck driver and the cleaner had to give such a statement. Did I go momentarily blind?

I read my statement as he had recorded it. I did not say anything and just signed it. After that, the police officer told me that they usually do not go to hotels to record statements. Either they would take the statement at the police station or in the hospital, but that he had made an exception for me as he knew I was friends with astrologer Pradhan and his family.

Later I was told that, when Abu, Suresh and Prakash went to the police station, the inspector first refused to come to the hotel to record the statement. They saw a book written by the famous astrologer Pradhan that was on the inspector's desk. In that book, my photograph had also appeared along with the photographs of many VIPs who knew Mr and Mrs Pradhan. When the inspector's attention was drawn to this, he opened the book. They showed him my photographs appearing alongside the family. That changed his mind and he agreed to come to the hotel to record my statement.

I signed my statement. They went back to the police station to complete formalities, to make a copy of the FIR and to make arrangements to get the car towed back to Bombay.

At around 4 p.m. Jaya asked me if I would be comfortable going to see the car. I asked "Why not? I am not scared. Let us go." The three of us – Jaya, Surekha and I – sat in an auto-rickshaw to go to the site of the accident. As we started, my heartbeat increased. I requested the driver to slow down. He inquired if I had a heart problem. I said no, but told him that I had met with an accident in the morning near Kamshet Ghat.

He stopped the auto, turned around to look at me and asked if it was me in the Maruti car. He said that he had seen that car and was sure that nobody could have survived that accident. I told him that it was me who was driving the car and that there were six of us in the car, but by the grace of God, everyone survived. After that, he drove at a slower pace.

We reached the accident spot. I was stunned to see that the front of the car including the doors were totally damaged. I could not believe that we were able to survive such an accident. I could not believe my eyes. Contrary to what I thought, it was a head-on collision.

My mind went blank – did I have momentary blindness? No, I was sure that there was no way a truck could come from the opposite direction when my car overturned.

A small crowd from the nearby village gathered. Two men inquired if I was driving the car. I told them that I was and why they were asking me. They pointed to a truck parked at a distance. One of them said that he was driving that truck. I looked straight into his eyes and asked their names. The driver who was also the owner of the truck said that his name was Muhammad and his cleaner's name is Hanuman.

I told him to forget the statement he had given to the police and that I needed the truth about what happened. I told him that as far as I was concerned, I did not see his truck at all. I told him that all this while I was under the impression that somebody banged my car from behind. I asked him if his view was the same.

I assured him that apart from the damage to my car no life was lost but that I needed to know the absolute truth in the name of God so that we know if any of us made mistakes that we can avoid in the future.

They looked at each other. The gathered crowd was silent. They were also waiting and wanting to know what Muhammad and Hanuman had to say.

After a long pause, Muhammad said, "I swear in the name of my God and Hanuman swears in the name of his God that we did not see your car coming head-on." He said that he felt the truck vibrate a bit and then he saw our car overturning in the rear-view mirror. They thought that we may have hit their truck.

He said that they waited at a distance. After a while they found their truck permit papers missing. So they went to the police station and complained. They found that there was no damage to the truck but a small portion of the mudguard had chipped. They did not know if it happened on that day or if it had chipped earlier.

An elderly person from among the villagers said, "You educated people would not believe this, but for the past few years on this three-kilometre stretch from Karla Caves to Kamshet Ghat, accidents happen once a week and result in at least one casualty. The only exception to that rule was today where no lives were lost."

As he finished, Abu, Suresh and Prakash, came with the Police Inspector to take my signature on certain documents. I told them exactly what the truck driver and his cleaner had told me. My brother-in-law Suresh, asked the inspector if he believed in ghosts. The Inspector said, "I know what exactly you want to say. I also know that both the parties have given false signed statements. They wanted to say they did not know what happened. I am tired of coming to this site and listening to the same statements from survivors over the past few years."

Well, what can we call this?

We reached Bombay around midnight and my home was packed with relatives and well-wishers. The next day, I called my friend who was with me in the car to find out if everything was fine with him and his family. He said that a detailed check-up revealed no serious injuries and no internal bleeding.

I asked him what he saw just before the car overturned. He said that though we were talking, his eyes were on the road and he did not see any vehicles coming towards us. He was sure that somebody hit us from behind. When I told him the facts he was stunned.

Another confirmation. I was convinced that a saviour is more powerful than a destroyer.

After this incident, Jaya, Rachana and Rachit prohibited me from driving by myself outside the city. I honoured their wishes.

As life went on, the frequency of visits to Pune reduced. Over the next two years, with the consent of the other two partners, we started winding down the Pune Stock Exchange operations due to a lack of time on everybody's part. Eventually, we settled our accounts.

CHAPTER FIFTY-NINE

On the family front, Rachana was in the final year of the MBA program. We started talking about wedding proposals for her but were unable to decide. Jaya and I decided to talk with Rachana about the various proposals. Jaya said that she would take the lead.

The next day when Rachana returned from college, Jaya discussed the matter with her. I did not know what transpired since I would come late from work. Jaya and I went for a morning walk the next day and she briefed me about her discussion with Rachana.

Rachana had asked her what would happen if she had someone in mind. She was going to speak with Jaya after Holashtak, as certain days before Holi are considered inauspicious.

She gave details of the boy. "His name is Ojas, he belongs to a Gujarati Vaishnav family, and was doing his MBA with her. He has come to our house with my other friends." I was surprised at my instant reaction when I said, "Okay, let us first meet the boy. Rachana is a mature adult. She must have looked into it from all angles. She is no more in her teens."

Rachana was anxious to know my reaction. I told her to speak to me when I returned from work. After dinner, the three of us sat down and I told her what I told Jaya. I said, "Let us meet the boy. But what if we do not approve of him? Or at a parental level, we disagree with Ojas's parents." Without hesitating, she said, "We have decided to go ahead only if both sets of parents agree."

It was Dhuleti, the festival of colours. Rachana suggested we meet Ojas at a restaurant near their college. She gave a precise description of Ojas and we were able to recognize him as he was waiting for us. We shook hands. It was 3 p.m. and the restaurant was not crowded.

We were uncertain about how to start the conversation. It was our first experience to meet any boy for matrimony reasons. I took the lead and said, "Look Ojas, what we will ask you would be a natural concern that any girl's parents will have. So be relaxed and let's talk as friends."

I asked about him and his family background. As our conversation progressed, we found him to be straightforward, forthcoming and honest. He never had any hesitancy in responding to our questions and did not even take a second to think.

Before parting, I asked him the same question that I had asked Rachana, "What if your parents do not agree to the match?" He replied instantly, "We will not go ahead if either set of parents are not convinced."

I asked him one final question, "Do you have any expectations?" Ojas asked, "What kind of expectations?"

I said, "Do you believe in the Dowry System?" He was just short of falling from his chair. He said, "Oh no! Absolutely no! We cannot even think about it."

Even today I regret asking him that question.

I told him "Okay, we will convey our decision to Rachana."

As we were driving home, Jaya and I discussed the meeting. The boy appeared well mannered, cultured, frank and honest. We did not feel like he was hiding anything. We were impressed. We also talked on the subject of his employment. I told Jaya, "I think we should see his potential, counting his educational background. I don't think we should even consider this while making our final decision." Jaya agreed. Both of us were perhaps thinking silently – 'What more could you ask of a son-in-law'?

When we got home, Rachana was eagerly awaiting our response. I told her, "We can meet his parents."

She immediately called Ojas. A parent level meeting was organized at the Sun and Sand Hotel in Juhu at its coffee shop. On the pre-decided date and time, we arrived at the same time as Ojas's parents.

After the initial pleasantries and ordering coffee and sandwiches, I told Udaybhai, Ojas's father about my family background. I told him about where I started my career, my UAE days, stock exchange brokerage business and current jewellery business. Udaybhai also gave his personal information about his family background, his professional activities, education and so on. The ladies, Jaya and Hansaben, listened silently.

We then began general talks and realized that we had identical thoughts on important topics such as children, ethics and life values. As we talked, we realized that sometimes we were even completing each other's sentences and thoughts. It did not feel like we were meeting for the first time.

After nearly an hour, I said, "*Saheb* (Sir), let us talk about the specific subject for which we have met today." Udaybhai said that his decision would be based on what we discussed. He said that he thought we had exchanged sufficient information and views to arrive at the decision, but that he was willing to provide references from the textile market, stock market and jewellery market.

I told him that I did not believe in checking with references on such delicate matters. This for the simple reason that we do not know who would give an honest opinion. What if the reference says, "Everything is fine, but…" I said, "My decision will be based on our talks today. Do you need any reference from me? Please tell me." He said, "No, my thinking is also the same."

We got up and came out to the hotel lobby. I extended my hand to say goodbye. Holding my hand, Udaybhai, asked, "How about coming home"? I responded, "*Saheb*, if you want to show us your house we do not want to see it. Houses are made of cement, sand, bricks and lime. But it turns into a home because of the people who live in it."

He immediately requested that we visit their home as a token of our new friendship. With that sentiment, I agreed.

We went to their house and met Ojas, his brother Anuj, and their aunt. Udaybhai perhaps wanted us to show us their house and their lifestyle. We never looked around the house. When Udaybhai invited us to take a look around the house, we politely declined.

On the way back, Jaya and I thought that this was the best proposal for Rachana that we could dream of. We were convinced and mentally prepared to go ahead should Udaybhai and their family also approve of us.

When we reached home, Ojas had already conveyed the message to Rachana that his parents appeared to be convinced. We too gave our nod to Rachana.

CHAPTER SIXTY

Rachana conveyed our decision to Ojas. The date was fixed for Rachana to meet Ojas's parents at their house. Rachana was happy. Jaya advised Rachana to be frank and honest about everything. She told her to be honest about how much (or little) cooking and housework she knew. She advised her to say exactly what she knew and what she did not.

After a few hours, Rachana came home after meeting Ojas's family. As soon as she stepped into the house, she said, "What Pappa, you conducted a thorough interview of Ojas, but I was not asked any specific question. We were just chatting." She continued, "On the contrary, Ojas's father said, today you will find everything fine with Ojas but if you want to know his weaknesses, ask us!"

Upon hearing the way the conversation went, our decision was further cemented. We were now waiting for Ojas's parents' decision. It came in a few days. They too had decided to move forward.

To work out the details of the engagement, we were invited to their house. Jaya instructed me not to eat or drink anything in their house, not even water, as per tradition. It is a tradition that I never believed in, but I had no option in the matter – these were Her Majesty's orders.

When we reached their home, we were accorded a warm and respectful welcome. We were offered water, snacks, and milk filled with almonds and pistachios. Jaya said, "We are sorry but, we cannot eat or drink anything in the home of our daughter's future in-laws." Ojas's parents tried to convince her but she would not budge. I kept quiet since I was given clear instructions.

Udaybhai told Jaya, "Jayaben, please show me even one sacred book in which it is written that you cannot have anything in your daughter's house? What you think is not a mandate given in any sacred books but is a conservative, traditional rule that is framed by society. I'll tell you why. In the olden days when the daughter's parents visited her in-laws' house, very naturally she would make a couple of dishes more and may be subject to taunts or sarcasm from her in-laws. To protect their daughter from such pain, society made a rule that no one should eat at their daughter's house. So the girl is not subjected to such taunts."

Jaya said, "Yes, that may be the reason, but we have seen our elders following the tradition. If we break the tradition, our elders will not appreciate it."

While they were talking a thought crossed my mind – what if elderly parents have only one daughter and no one else to look after them?

Udaybhai said, "I have a question for you. Now that we are moving ahead with our relationship, tell me, will Rachana be our daughter or not?"

"Of course, she will," Jaya responded.

"And will Ojas be your son or not?" he asked.

"Yes, indeed!" she replied.

"Now you tell me, who is from the girl's side – you or us?" Udaybhai rested his case.

It was a masterstroke. Jaya had no answer. I finally intervened and told her that it was okay for us to eat what was offered to us and that we should not resist any further.

Ever since that day, even until today, we go to their house, eat, and even comfortably stay with them for a few days. More than being the in-laws of our respective children, we enjoy each other's company as brothers, sisters and friends.

Over the years, I have learned to address each issue independently on its merit. It cannot simply be black or white.

The engagement and marriage dates were fixed. All of us agreed that the celebrations would be simple and graceful. We agreed that we would avoid being extravagant and not spend unnecessarily on things such as decorations. Every decision was taken and implemented with mutual consent.

After their wedding, Ojas got a job transfer to the USA. He left and Rachana joined him after three months. We parents, continue to enjoy ourselves in each other's company. We share almost everything and our lives have become an open book to each other.

CHAPTER SIXTY-ONE

While everything seemed to be going well, I still felt that I was not happy. It seemed to be stress. I could recognize the anxiety having dealt with this in the past. Recognition is the first step to resolution. Once I was able to understand myself, I knew it was of paramount importance to take remedial steps to avoid it getting out of control.

Coincidentally during that time, I was reading Stephen Covey's book *The Seven Habits of Highly Effective People*.

In that book, I came across a sentence which transformed my attitude towards myself – "Whatever situation you are in today, it is because you have taken that decision yesterday." This sentence resonated deeply within me and my attitude changed. I stopped complaining and worrying about circumstances that were caused due to my own decisions in the past. So, if the outcome of the decision was not what I had originally desired, there was no one else to blame for it.

Once I digested this philosophy that decisions are not right or wrong, although the outcomes may not be what we want, I felt relaxed, calmer and more cheerful.

In the meantime, our son, Rachit, was mapping his career path. Until he completed his graduation, I felt like we never seriously discussed his career. I thought that I had failed as a father to an extent. Rachana had done her MBA after graduation, and Rachit followed suit.

Fortunately, Rachana had already set a benchmark for him, and his goal was at least to match it.

However, while he was doing his MBA, I was able to talk to him on various issues including his career. He indicated that he was not interested in the business. I presumed his goal was to become an executive in a firm after he completed his course.

Rachana was not able to start her MBA for two years after her commerce graduation due to my stubborn thinking. By the time Rachit finished his college graduation, my thinking on higher education had undergone a drastic change. I became a staunch proponent that both girls and boys should at a minimum have a Master's degree.

Now that I had come out of my self-imposed depressed days, I was able to apply my mind to Rachit's future. I felt guilty that I could not do the same with Rachana.

I discovered many other qualities in Rachit. In studies, he was doing exceedingly well. He was the editor of his college magazine; he was participating in intercollegiate debates and won several awards for his college. At the same time, he continued to keep himself updated on cricket and other sports, Bollywood, and vivid cultural activities. Just like his sister, I found him to be extremely intelligent, kind-hearted and emotional.

Rachit completed his MBA with flying colours and topped his college. He received a job offer after a campus interview. We were all happy. I asked him once again whether he was interested in joining the jewellery business or the stock market brokerage business. He said, "No Pappa, I aim to study further after gaining some work experience." Jaya and I decided to honour his wish.

CHAPTER SIXTY-TWO

It was just over a year since Rachana and Ojas had moved to the USA. My father-in-law (*Dada*), mother-in-law (*Aai*) and sister-in-law (Surekha) applied for and got a visa to visit the USA. This encouraged Jaya and me to get one too.

We decided to visit the USA together with a stopover in Hong Kong on the onward journey, and in Bangkok on our return.

We consulted Rachana, Ojas, my other sister-in-law Kishori (Jaya's younger sister) and my sister Pramila, who were already in the USA about their convenience. All of them were happy to know about our plans to make this trip. With that, we started our preparations to leave.

In those days, most passengers, depending on the airline, were allowed to carry two bags of 32 kg each plus a cabin bag of about 10 kg. We made the most of this baggage allowance – and packed a full 10 bags plus four cabin bags, three ladies' handbags and one shoulder bag. We had excess baggage – about seven to eight kgs in total. As a result, we had to remove several items at the Bombay Airport.

Our first stopover was in Hong Kong. We had already booked a hotel with airport transfer arrangements. Visa was on arrival. After clearing Immigration and Customs, we collected our bags. Somehow, we managed to fit our luggage into two trolleys.

I was searching for a placard with my name on it, as I was promised. When I found it, I saw the person rushing to us impatiently. He screamed, "Come fast, all other passengers are waiting."

He looked at both the trolleys with amazement and asked whether the luggage was all ours. We said yes. I told him that while making hotel reservations with airport transfers, I had informed the agency about the number of items we had. He said that he did not know about that, and anyway these bags would not fit into his bus as it was a passenger bus and not a cargo bus!

Before I could say anything he almost yelled, "You need a truck!!" He conveyed his intentions loud and clear. Wasting no time, I asked him, "What options do you suggest?" He said that I could either keep the extra bags in the luggage locker room at the airport or hire taxis. I asked how many he could accommodate. He said he could take one bag per person plus one cabin bag each.

I asked him to guide us to the luggage locker, which he did. We paid a deposit of about 750 Hong Kong dollars (HKD), with the balance due at the time of check out.

We reached the hotel. After the checking-in formalities, we went to our allotted rooms. We were thirsty after the journey. There was no drinking water in the room. When I called housekeeping they said that we could drink from the tap directly or buy bottled water from the store on the ground floor. I asked him how safe it was to drink tap water. He responded that generally, no one worried about it since it was safe. He added, "You seem to be new to international travel."

I realized that we had not done any homework on our trip to the USA, including preparing ourselves for travel-related rules and hassles.

After drinking water and eating the food we had carried with us, I went to see the bell captain. He was a young talkative boy. He got friendly with me in a few minutes. We gave him a box of *Kaju Katli* (Indian sweet with cashews). He was happy. I explained our baggage situation to him. He checked on the computer and said that there was no such special mention recorded at the time of making a reservation, otherwise they would have made arrangements. Instead of arguing with him, I asked him for his help and suggestion on what to do.

He said that if we hired a taxi the next day, he would give us some room in the hotel storage area for free, as our rooms were not large enough. The taxi fare to and from the airport would be 300 HKD. Despite this, we would save 400 HKD.

The next day we rented a taxi, went to the airport which was about 25 miles from the hotel. Before checking out our bags, and having learnt my lesson at Bombay airport, I thought of going to the airline counter to enquire about baggage rules. The lady behind the counter listened to me attentively. The rules were different in Hong Kong. They wanted each bag to be 32 kg, instead of a collective total. So for example, if we had 30 kg in one and 34 kg in another bag, we would have to pay for two extra kgs (at 750 HKD per kg). I was glad I asked.

I transferred the bags to the hotel. We spent about four hours balancing the five bags with 32 kg in each and no more than 10 kg in the cabin bags, leaving space for shopping. We bought one more cabin bag in Hong Kong.

Once we settled the logistical issues, we enjoyed our stay in Hong Kong. From there, we flew to Los Angeles. We spent about three weeks in LA. Our itinerary was LA-Florida-New York-Cincinnati-LA-Bombay. We had purchased a VUSA ticket. One of the conditions of this ticket was having to adhere to the date and the itinerary. The domestic travel rules were strict as well. To avoid any further issues, as a precautionary measure, we shipped two bags by FedEx from LA to Cincinnati, where Rachana and Ojas lived.

CHAPTER SIXTY-THREE

We arrived in Florida. We were surprised that most people at the airport were not fluent in English. They were speaking another language which we later came to know was Spanish – yet another evidence of my not doing enough homework and not knowing this fact. We had rented an SUV (like a minivan) to make sure that all of our luggage fit.

With the help of one of our American clients, we had booked our stay at the International Society for Krishna Consciousness (ISKCON). It provided lodging for its members worldwide. We opted for it for a couple of reasons – 1. We were vegetarian. Four out of the five of us did not eat onion or garlic and my in-laws did not like to eat at a restaurant. 2. We had seen the residence facility at ISKCON Bombay which was world-class. We thought that America would certainly have better facilities. Therefore, ISKCON seemed to be the perfect place for us.

We arrived only to be jolted and shocked. The property was spread over a small area, absolutely no comparison to the one in Bombay. There was no multi-story building in and around the vicinity. The building was just the ground floor, almost like a barrack. People around us spoke Spanish. There was no separate structure where guests could stay. I went to meet the President of the temple. He informed me that he had not received any communication about our visit. He too was not fluent in spoken English. Since I knew that I could not simply hire a cab and go to a hotel, I wondered what to do. Additionally, it was also getting dark. I requested, rather pleaded, with the President to help us out. He said that they had no facilities for guests but asked us to wait while he checked if something could be done.

He came back in a few minutes and said that he was able to arrange for a room where the ladies could stay, along with the luggage. The men would have to sleep in the dormitory along with other male disciples. The Men's toilets did not have doors, but just 3/4th curtains.

We had no option but to accept whatever makeshift facilities were offered. We dragged the bags to the room that they vacated for us and found ourselves sitting on the bags as the room was so small. There was just one single bed in the corner. It was already one hour after sunset and we had no option but to pray to God for a miracle, as there was no way that even three women would be able to fit in the room.

While we wondered how we were going to adjust, a lady came and announced that they were arranging for a bigger room. It was obvious that to accommodate us, one more family must have volunteered to be inconvenienced.

We decided to be ready for any adjustments without further expectations. We went to the family who was vacating their room for us, thanked them and apologized for the inconvenience we had caused.

The room was just about enough for us to sleep overnight. The next morning we woke up fresh, reconciled to stay in those conditions for three more days. We did *darshan*.

I got ready and looked for conducted city tours. This was then that we learnt that the location was far from downtown where all the tours started.

Once again, I went to the temple President. After thanking him for making arrangements for our stay of three days, he started talking. He educated us that Spanish was the second language in the USA, especially in certain parts of the West Coast and in the South. I briefed him about this being our first visit to the USA. He agreed we did not do enough homework. I requested his help to arrange for a conducted tour for two days. He thought for a while and said, "Okay, I will give you the temple van and driver after 2 p.m." It was already noon by then.

We had *Prasad* (lunch) at the temple. Exactly at 2 p.m., we went to the van, and the driver was waiting for us. He asked us questions in Spanish. We replied in English, explaining to him that we wished to go sightseeing. We were speaking two different languages.

After a few attempts at conversation, I got down and went to the President to explain to him about the communication issue. I was concerned that if we do not understand each other, then simple things like directions would be misunderstood. He nodded and immediately called for one disciple who understood and spoke some English. I told him that we wanted to see Miami Beach, National Park, and Orlando. He explained to us that we could not see everything in one day due to the distances.

We picked a couple of places to visit. Both our guides made our tour enjoyable. We became friendlier with each passing hour. We came back in the evening. By now we were reconciled to the accommodation and had adjusted to the facilities provided. Their concern, love and respect were endearing.

The next morning, after we did *Arti* (prayer), two female disciples came and lay face down at our feet. They were flat on the floor (called *Sashtang Dandavat*). They exclaimed, "We are so fortunate to have you here. You are from the land of Lord Krishna." At first, we felt proud of being Indian and the respect that we received. The next moment, we were embarrassed and ashamed – we had done nothing to deserve this.

Aai, Surekha and Jaya expressed their desire to the temple disciples to permit them to prepare *Prasad*. Permission was instantly granted.

They had to bathe again before the kitchen was handed over to them. The news spread across the campus like wildfire – Indian *Prasad* for the deity prepared by Indians today. All the residents were excited.

In the next two and half hours, *Prasad* was ready. As the ladies were coming out of the kitchen, they were informed that Lord Krishna was served juice and soup every day. They went back into the kitchen and prepared it. We went for *darshan*. After this, the *Prasad* was arranged for everyone to eat. Just as the ladies were beginning to come out, the disciples informed them that since they had prepared the *Prasad*, they would have to clean the utensils in the kitchen as well.

A long queue of about 50 devotees waited patiently for their *Prasad*. The ladies went into the kitchen, cleaned all the utensils used, and arranged them as guided. When they came out from the kitchen, they were surprised and touched to find out that not a single person had started taking the *Prasad*. Everyone was waiting for them to come and join them. "Wasn't this a way of Indian culture?" they asked.

Everyone appreciated the delicious *Prasad*. The ladies had made friends with the other women there. It is said that when food becomes *Prasad* it is always delicious.

After *Prasad*, again at 2 p.m., we got to the temple van for more sightseeing with our two friends. That day we left it to them to take us where they wanted to. We were having a nice time. Before we realized it, it was 5 p.m. I found that both our friends were worried and talking in

Spanish. I could sense that they were discussing a serious problem.

When I asked them, the English-speaking friend told us, "I think we have missed the way to the freeway. This area is notorious. You can see that all the shops are closed and boarded. No one is walking on the street. Now only Lord Krishna can save us." I asked him, why people were so scared even in daylight. He informed us sombrely that they had heard that the area had gangsters who came onto the street after 5 p.m. and looted and killed people.

"May Lord Krishna save us," they both chanted, "Hare Krishna, Hare Krishna!"

By now, we were all worried. Looking around I spotted a gas station and asked them to check at the convenience store there. We drove up to the store. The door was locked, but on one side we found a small window that was slightly open. We knocked. In Spanish, our guides explained that we had lost our way. The window shutter went up just a bit. The man behind the window gave us quick directions and pulled the shutter down. We started for the Temple. Everyone was tense for about 10 minutes until we reached the freeway. Our English-speaking friend jumped with joy and declared loudly, "We are saved! We are saved by Lord Krishna. Hare Krishna, Hare Krishna (Hail Lord Krishna)!"

The next morning, I requested the temple President to arrange a cab to take us to the airport. He said that our two friends who drove us sightseeing insisted on dropping us off at the airport. We thanked him and started to load our bags into the van. A few female disciples signalled to us, and in Spanish said, "Please don't go!"

We told them (through our English speaking friend) that we too felt like staying back, but our onward journey and itinerary was booked and could not be changed, unfortunately.

When the van started moving, we saw the male disciples waving at us and a few female disciples crying. They followed us up to the gate of the campus.

Our experience at ISKCON, Florida, which began with a deep disappointment ended with unforgettable memories. It is hard to describe the feeling in words except to say that it was different from anything we had experienced before. Maybe we could call it divine.

CHAPTER SIXTY-FOUR

Our flight from Florida to New York was at 1:30 p.m. We boarded the flight. It left the gate, was on the runway but did not take off. All passengers wondered what the problem was. Turned out there was a technical problem with the aircraft. After about an hour on the tarmac, the aircraft returned to the gate. We disembarked. A while later, they announced that a part in the aircraft needed to be replaced. The new departure time was 6 p.m. We were each given $10. At 6 p.m. they announced another delay, this time a departure time of 8 p.m. As an alternative, passengers could make bookings for the next morning, with overnight accommodation in the hotel provided by the airline.

I went to the counter and asked the agent to book us for the next morning if the departure was delayed beyond 8 p.m. He said that he had noted it in the system. We were keen to fly even if it was late since Rachana and Ojas may have already reached New York and booked a rental car for us from the airport to ISKCON where they would be waiting for us to join them. We calculated that if the flight took off at say 8:30 p.m., we would reach New York airport by 11 p.m. Cell phones were not common in those days, so we had no means of contacting Rachana and Ojas. We tried calling at 7 p.m. but were unable to get through, maybe because it was *Arti* time at ISKCON.

At 7:30 p.m. they announced that the flight was ready to take off. We already had boarding cards. The flight finally took off at 8:45 p.m. We reached New York at 11:30 p.m. and collected our luggage. We exited to check if Rachana and Ojas were there just in case. Expectedly, they were not. I also looked around to see if anyone was standing with a placard bearing my name. Not finding anyone, I called ISKCON and luckily someone picked up the phone. Unfortunately, the accent was so heavy that I could not follow immediately. By the time I figured it out, the telephone was disconnected.

As we wondered what to do next, a gentleman came to check with us if we needed a taxi. I explained to him about our number of bags and where we wanted to go. He said that was not a problem if we paid $35 plus toll. I agreed. He asked us to wait, saying he would be back soon.

Just as he left, Jaya told me that a gentleman speaking in Hindi told her and Surekha, *"Behenji, uske saath aap mat jaiye. Raste mein aapko pareshan karega."* meaning, "Sister, do not go with that person. He will create problems for you on the way."

As soon as she finished, the person who offered us a taxi came back. He said that we would need two cars. I took the opportunity to thank him, and told him that

I was not interested. He went back. Then I went to the person who told Jaya and Surekha to be careful. I asked him, "Thank you for alerting us. What is the alternative?" He suggested that we take an airport taxi managed by the cops, most likely a large Dodge van. Thanking him, I showed him the address where we wanted to go. I also asked him for a favour – to call ISKCON to inform Rachana and Ojas that we had landed and that once we got a cab, we would be on the way.

He asked me to dial from the payphone, which I did. Up until now, he was speaking in Hindi or English with an Indian accent. He suddenly switched to a heavy American English accent on the phone. I confess I might have followed less than 50% of what he said. Anyway, it seemed like the message was conveyed. We could relax. As he was guiding us to the airport taxi queue, he warned us, "Be careful when you are in the taxi. Roll up your windows and make sure doors are properly locked. Sometimes even airport taxi drivers are hand in glove with private taxi operators. They stop the taxis in the middle of nowhere, either to frighten you or to extract more money or to force you to hire a private taxi. I am cautioning you just in case. If you encounter any trouble, keep my business card. Tell the driver my name and number. Most taxi drivers know that I belong to the intelligence unit at the airport. In all probability, you will not need to use my name and number, but it is better to remain alert." I asked him where he was originally from.

He said, "Punjab." He made us wait in the queue and talked to a police officer who was managing the location of taxis. We again thanked him.

It took a while to get a big Dodge van taxi. Finally, we got it at 12:45 a.m. With the luggage, we barely managed to squeeze ourselves into the taxi. I handed over the address to the driver. He drove for about 15 minutes on a road without street lights. Suddenly, he stopped the cab. He flashed a light on the address saying, "Oh God, I have taken the opposite direction." I asked him to turn around. He said we would need to again pass by the airport. I said that was fine. He asked if I would give him a nice tip. I agreed.

He made a U-turn. We passed by the airport from where we boarded the taxi. Suddenly, he started talking, "Where are you visiting from?"

I responded, "California."

He interjected, "No I am asking you, where have you have come from?"

I reiterated, "California. My sister is there."

He went on, "No I am asking which country are you from?"

Seeing no point in resisting him, given it was past 1 a.m. I said, "India."

"Where in India are you from?"

From his accent, I guessed he was an Egyptian thanks to my stay in Dubai for more than seven years where I interacted with people from many nationalities.

"Bombay," I responded.

"Where in Bombay?" he asked.

I was surprised. "Are you aware of Bombay geography?"

He responded, "Yes, I know Colaba, Byculla, Malad."

I started feeling more at ease, relaxed and above all safe.

Curious, I asked him, "How do you know all these names?"

"Where are you are from?" he pressed.

I said, "I am from Ghatkopar."

He went on, "I stayed in Bombay for seven years."

"How come?" I asked.

"I was with the Egyptian Navy. In that connection, I spent time with Indian Navy personnel. Most of the years I was around Navy Nagar."

Hearing this, I was now completely relaxed, not panicky anymore. I continued the conversation, "Good to know. Did you like Bombay?"

"Yes, I enjoyed it there. I saw many movies starring Rajesh Khanna."

Rajesh Khanna was a big superstar then. "*Chal, Chal, Chal, Mere Hathi*", he started singing this famous Hindi film song.

"Do you still see Hindi movies?" I asked.

"Hardly."

We reached a toll plaza and had to pay $4.

I checked with Jaya, Surekha, *Aai* and *Dada* if any of them had any change. No one did. Reluctantly, I pulled out my wallet, noticing that he was looking from the corner of his eyes at it. I deliberately murmured, "We are tourists. We do not carry much cash."

I pulled out a $20 bill and handed it over to him saying, "Keep the change with you to pay at any other tolls. We will account for it at the end."

He said, "OK. Will you give me a tip?"

I answered in the affirmative and asked him how much more time it would take to reach.

He responded, "About 15 mins. You will surely give me a tip, right?"

Two more toll stations came on the way. At both points, he would stop and ask if we would give him a good tip. I kept reassuring him I would.

After about 15 minutes, he again stopped and asked, "Will you give me a good tip for sure?" I told him, "Sure, I have already told you so."

He took a left turn and in less than a minute, he stopped the cab to say, "Here you go. We reached."

I knocked on the door. Rachana and Ojas opened it. They were waiting in the lobby. The driver helped us unload the luggage. I gave him a $15 tip. He was happy, thanked us, and was on his way.

CHAPTER SIXTY-FIVE

ISKCON in New York was a multi-storied structure with much better facilities than the one in Florida. We were allotted one big room with seven beds, three of them being bunk beds. While in New York, we saw major tourist attractions like the Statue of Liberty, Empire State Building and World Trade Centre Twin Towers. We got a feeling of Bombay while there.

Rachana told us that she had received the two bags shipped by FedEx. Both the bags were placed in a big cardboard box without any handle to lift them. When the delivery person came to deliver it at their Cincinnati apartment, Ojas was at work. Rachana was alone. The man came and asked if there was anyone who could help him lift the box. Rachana said, 'I can' not knowing what the box looked like. He looked at her and smiled. He said, "Don't worry." When he brought in the box, Rachana saw him perspiring. Worried he might faint, she offered him water or a soft drink. This was yet another example of our unpreparedness.

We were on the third floor at ISKCON New York. Our room window was opened halfway with the help of a thick stick, to allow fresh air. Rachana and Ojas had gone out to explore the city. We were tired and opted to rest. As we were talking, we heard a knock on the door. Not a knock, but someone frantically banging it. I immediately opened the door to see a young girl, looking visibly frightened and trembling. I asked, "Yes?" She snapped, "Did you drop a coffee glass jar?" I said, "No, we were just talking." She said, "A glass bottle just touched my dress. If it had fallen on my head, it would have killed me. If I had called the police, they would have closed all ISKCON Temples," she said, still trembling.

Confused and concerned, I looked at the others. No one seemed to understand what she was saying and why. At that moment, all we could do was to reassure her saying, "We will certainly take care." She started to cry and dramatically said, "I was saved by Lord Krishna."

After she left, Surekha lifted the curtain as she remembered a coffee bottle had been kept near the partially open window. When she lifted the curtain, we discovered that the bottle was not there. What happened now made sense. I immediately went downstairs. Thankfully, she was still in the lobby. She was a disciple. I apologized profusely explaining how we found that our bottle had indeed fallen from the window of our room. She simply said, "It is fine, take care next time. Today Lord Krishna saved me."

I am intentionally providing a detailed account of such memorable incidents instead of describing the places we visited. That is because anyone in a similar situation reading this may benefit from learning how I reacted.

Our trip to New York was coming to an end. Rachana and Ojas' flights were from a different New York airport. They had planned the trip in such a way that they would reach Cincinnati half an hour ahead of us.

We reached the airport and presented ourselves at the check-in counter. The counter attendant asked for our passports, which she verified and returned to us. After a few clicks on her computer, she looked up telling us, "Oh, you cannot travel to Cincinnati. Your booking is cancelled. My computer shows that you are still in Florida."

I was puzzled wondering, 'What exactly does she mean? Weren't we in New York? Standing right in front of her?' Bewildered, I asked, "Ma'am, we are standing here in front of you, how come you think we are still in Florida?"

She responded, "That I don't know. My computer says that you have not yet flown out of Florida." After arguing a little bit, I asked her if I could talk to a manager. She directed me to a gentleman standing nearby. I asked him if he could help me out. After checking the computer he said, "I would say the computer says you are still in Florida." I responded, "That is what the lady at the counter also told me. I have come to you to help us out and put us on this flight." He said, "It is not possible since your booking is cancelled."

I suddenly remembered that I had saved the boarding cards for the Miami-New York flight. I pulled them out and showed them to him. He too was puzzled. Then I speculated what might have happened. "There may be some error on the part of the counter staff at Miami to whom I requested to put us on the next day's flight if the scheduled flight did not take off by 8 p.m."

We were asked to wait. I went to him twice in 30 minutes to check the status and possibility of putting us on the same flight. He got irritated, asking in an unfriendly if not humiliating tone, "Do you want to fly or not?" I was also irritated by now, "Okay, so now you are the boss. Do what you can do. I will see what I have to do." He immediately got defensive and told me, "No, I didn't mean it that way."

In the next 10 minutes, he called me again. "I will put three of you on this flight and others on the next flight which is after two hours." I agreed realizing that at least three of us would now be able to fly and meet Rachana and Ojas at the airport. While printing the boarding passes, one more seat opened up and so four of us could now be on the same flight. I opted to wait and take the next flight. I accompanied the others to their gate. Just as boarding was about to begin, I heard my name being called, asking me to meet a gate agent.

When I met him he asked me if I would also like to go on this flight. I nodded. He issued me a fresh boarding pass in exchange for one on the next flight. And so all of us were off to Cincinnati.

We enjoyed our stay in Cincinnati, visiting a few tourist attractions from there including Niagara Falls. Jaya and I had our first pizza while we were there. I wondered how we could even justify making this trip because Rachana and Ojas were still trying to settle in the US. To their great credit, they did not make us feel uncomfortable, even for a second.

We returned to California to take a flight back to Bombay, this time with a stopover in Bangkok. Before we left, Jaya and I thought that if Rachit wanted to come to the USA to pursue his Master's, it would be worthwhile. We decided to encourage him.

CHAPTER SIXTY-SIX

We arrived in Bombay after an eventful trip. I had learned many lessons as the trip organizer.

Upon returning, we asked Rachit, who was by now working in ICICI Bank, whether he wished to study in the USA. He said, "Yes, but how will we arrange the funds?" It would cost us nearly 80,000-90,000 US Dollars for a two-year MBA program. I told Rachit, "You prepare to go, we will do some research." We had already discussed this with Rachana and Ojas. They liked the idea and insisted Rachit do his MBA in the USA.

In the meanwhile, Ojas's younger brother, Anuj, was also preparing to pursue a Master's in Computer Engineering in the US. Udaybhai was aware of all the requirements. Anuj left for the USA.

After he left, we again spoke to Rachana and Ojas. They convinced us that Rachit would have a bright future there. They told us not to worry about anything, they would take care of his education.

We talked to Udaybhai and Hansaben about Rachit's intentions of going to the USA for his MBA. We expressed our concern about arranging funds, even though Rachana and Ojas had asked us not to worry about that.

Without any hesitation, Udaybhai, sincerely, said, "We are one family. It is Rachana and Ojas' duty to organize everything for Rachit as they did for Anuj. I am sure Rachit will have a bright future in the USA. I am convinced he is destined to do something big."

Jaya and I looked at him with gratitude. We were speechless.

We considered disposing of our Pune flat at Koregaon Park which we had purchased because of my weekly visits to Pune.

We calculated and recalculated. Still, we would be short of the requisite funds. We always kept Udaybhai and Hansaben in the loop, never hesitating to share our financial position with them. Udaybhai would always say, "Don't worry. We will pull it off together as a family." Hansaben would always endorse it as well. Their words were always spoken with utmost sincerity. They meant every word of what they said.

Once, over dinner at their home, Udaybhai asked Rachit how far he had reached in his preparation to go to the USA. Rachit answered, "Uncle, I don't get any time to prepare for even GMAT and TOEFL which is the basic requirement to apply for admission to any university." Udaybhai encouraged him, "Rachit, you are already a professional. You should learn to ride more than two horses at a time. I am sure you can and will do it."

With Udaybhai's constant push and encouragement, Rachana and Ojas's guidance and insistence, Rachit finally cleared his GMAT and TOEFL with good scores. He began applying to US universities.

We sold our Pune flat and some investments to make whatever provision we could. We left the rest to the confidence of Udaybhai, Hansaben, Rachana and Ojas.

By the time Rachit left for the USA, I lost my parents.

Rachit got admission into The Ohio State University in Columbus, approximately 90 miles from Rachana and Ojas's home in Cincinnati. They recommended sending Rachit a few weeks ahead of his orientation so that he could get familiar with American culture and look for campus jobs. He went a month ahead. Rachana and Ojas managed to get him a credit card, helped him rent a sharing apartment and also met his roommate to make sure that their temperament matched.

We knew Rachit was actively looking for an on-campus job. He would go from department to department to find a job vacancy. He picked up a small job including working as an index card sorter in the library and another as a student-athlete tutor. His roommate always complained about Rachit's food habits – eating only frozen mac and cheese every day. He was concerned it would affect his health. Rachit was conscious of every dollar he spent.

Just as his first-quarter fees were paid by Rachana and Ojas, he got a job in the Treasury Department with a stipend of $900 per month and his entire fees paid for. Even though he had to work 20 hours a week, this was as close to a scholarship as possible.

We were happy and relieved. We wondered how we would ever repay Rachana and Ojas, Udaybhai and Hansaben, for their feelings, confidence and encouragement. No, never, we shall always be indebted to them.

CHAPTER SIXTY-SEVEN

One year after Rachit went there, we visited the US again. Rachit was with Rachana and Ojas for the weekend. We saw he had lost a lot of weight. We drove from Cincinnati to Columbus to Rachit's apartment. His apartment did not have any furniture, not even a table or a chair. But it was spacious and carpeted. Rachana and Ojas assured us that this was a typical student residence. His living condition was much better than other students. His roommate had gone to California to stay with his sister. We stayed with Rachit for a month or so.

While he was at college, every morning we used to go for a walk. I happened to go alone one day when I saw a sign for a 'Garage Sale'. Not familiar with what that was, out of curiosity, I went to look, inquiring about the prices. I saw a round plastic dining table and six chairs for $16. I thought it would serve a dual purpose – to use a dining table and to use the chairs for sitting. I requested the man who was selling to help me drop these items at our residence on the next street. He was a bit hesitant. I explained to him that we were on a visit staying with our son who was doing his MBA at OSU. He looked at me and in a kind tone, said, "Ok, let us go." He dropped the chairs and fixed the table for us. While leaving, he gave us a friendly smile. I could not figure out what he was trying to convey with his smile.

Rachit returned that evening and was happy to see the additions to the house. But he also said, "Pappa, was it necessary to spend $16?" Jaya told him, "Rachit, let us also feel that we have done something. Do not worry."

The following week, we invited Rachit's friends over for dinner. Jaya made *idli, sambar and pav vada* – the most sought after street foods in Bombay. They commented, "We are eating homemade Indian food after almost a year." More than them, Jaya and I were happy and satisfied.

Meanwhile, Rachana had settled into her post-MBA job. Ojas was also progressing with his. We came back to Bombay, satisfied with where things stood for our family.

Rachit graduated. While we were not able to attend Rachana's graduation, we wanted to attend at least his. Unfortunately, we were not able to go. Even today, I regret not being able to attend both their graduation ceremonies. It was a proud moment for them. After all, they had slogged to see that day. They deserved for us to be there with them. Sorry, Rachana. Sorry, Rachit. But our reasons were more than one.

I do not want to keep looking back. If I continue to do that, I will not be able to look ahead.

Now, it was time for Rachit to find a job. Like him, we were also anxious. While we were with Rachana for a couple of months, we had heard some horrific tales of students not getting suitable jobs in line with their qualifications. Some of them had to go back to their home country. I couldn't imagine the disappointment of those students and their parents, many of whom had to take a loan to pursue their further studies.

Rachit was fortunate. So were we. After all his hard work, Rachana and Ojas's unconditional loving support, Udaybhai and Hansaben's blessings, and well wishes of all near and dear ones, he found a job.

Congratulations started pouring in. With his sincerity, honesty, and hard work, we were confident of him climbing his career path. Udaybhai was even more confident than us.

Now was the time for him to get married. We felt it was enough of bachelorhood for Rachit. He had passed his SSC, completed his graduation and post-graduation in India and worked immediately after for three years. Then he went to the USA to do an MBA again, worked there while studying, and immediately started working there again. Was there enough time at his disposal to enjoy at all?

We started receiving many marriage proposals for him, but he maintained that he first wished to build up some capital in the USA as he had made up his mind to settle there. We tried to convince him but did not want to pressurize him beyond a point.

He never even spelt out his preference on a life partner. But Jaya and I had. In our mind, his life partner had to be a graduate, without much gap between their educations. She should have the potential to study in the USA if needed. Temperaments of both the families must generally match to avoid the boy and girl getting squeezed between parents. The family need not be affluent but should be cultured, vegetarian, and have some social standing. None of the proposals we received met these conditions. We did not even mention most of them to Rachit.

Then one day, we received a proposal from a known, respected family. The girl had completed her graduation in commercial arts/graphic design, from a highly reputed college in Bombay. We fixed a time to meet the girl and her parents.

By this time, Rachana and Ojas had moved to Chicago. They were blessed with a son, Parth, our first grandchild.

We wished for Rachit to get married and raise his family. We talked to him about this proposal. He remembered the family but did not recall ever meeting the girl, even when they were younger. We also discussed this with Rachana and Ojas. They suggested we meet her and if we were satisfied we would all try to convince Rachit.

We met in a restaurant. I will admit this time around I was a little more relaxed than when meeting Ojas. Perhaps I was more experienced by now. Our association with Udaybhai and Hansaben had also taught us a great many things about how to deal with such delicate situations.

Her name was Poonam. After a routine exchange of pleasantries, I initiated a conversation with her and asked, "Poonam, is it okay if we can chat as friends?"

"Sure, uncle," she politely responded.

"How far do you think you can go ahead in your career with the qualifications that you have?"

"There is a lot more I can do." She went on to explain in detail how her Commercial Art, Graphic Designing and flair for photography would help build her career.

I asked her, "What if your life partner asked you not to work?"

She said, "It is okay. After all, whatever I have to do in future will have to be with mutual consent."

I thought she passed my first test.

I continued, "I am casually asking you, but suppose you have to travel a lot with your life partner from city to city, country to country, how would you take it?"

She confidently replied, "I will be fine. I like travelling and where we stay is our home."

I went on, "What if he gets stuck in one place where no travelling is required?"

She said, "That is also fine. We would be living in our home. I have been staying in Bombay since birth."

We found Poonam to be sober, straightforward, intelligent and cultured. She perhaps passed my final test.

We then had a general chat and parted. I was careful about not raising Poonam and her parents' hopes at that time.

Jaya and I returned home confident that this was the girl. We would be looking forward to Rachit's views. We briefed Rachana, Ojas, Rachit. And of course, Udaybhai and Hansaben.

One day when Udaybhai and Hansaben were visiting us, I asked Poonam's parents if she could come to meet them. They agreed without hesitation. Udaybhai and Hansaben also liked Poonam.

When Rachana and Ojas visited, we all once again met Poonam with her parents. After meeting them, Rachana and Ojas were on the same page as us. They said they would also try to convince Rachit to at least make a short trip and meet Poonam and her parents, Rekhaben and Nareshbhai.

We pressed Rachit hard on the phone to come to Bombay. He finally gave us his date of travel. I conveyed and updated Rekhaben and Nareshbhai. Jaya and I told them that now it was in the hands of our children. Let them meet. Let them decide. Both have an equal right of saying no. At least we were confident, that would not happen.

But just a week before he was scheduled to arrive, Rachit gave us a shock. He was cancelling his trip because of some urgent assignment given to him in the office. The first thought that crossed my mind was that it was a pretext to delay coming. Jaya and I were completely disappointed. We had to convey and update Poonam's parents. They too sounded somewhat disappointed.

I told Jaya that it seemed as if Rachit was avoiding visiting. I suggested that she make a trip to the USA to convince him and impress upon his necessity to take a decision. It was not good for us to keep anyone waiting indefinitely. Jaya agreed. I was confident that Rachit would listen to his mother. I always thought him to be a 'Mama's boy'.

Two weeks after Jaya's departure, Nareshbhai came to meet me. He told me, "We have received a couple of more proposals for Poonam. Any idea when Rachit will come?" I told him, "No, so far he has not given any indication on a definite date." I added, "If you find other proposals are good enough to seriously look at, I would say please go ahead, as I am amenable to give you a clear picture."

After a week, Nareshbhai and I met again. "I spoke with my daughter. It appears that she is inclined to go for Rachit first," he conveyed.

I was upfront with him, "Let us be clear. I am not able to give you any time limit, but we will try to come to a decision as soon as we can."

Meanwhile, I happened to attend Poonam's parents' silver wedding anniversary. I met Poonam and asked her if she had remained connected with Rachit through email. She said, "Uncle, he is not regular in responding but I understand. Auntie is there and she should be his priority." I thanked her for understanding.

As I had hoped, Jaya was able to convince Rachit. They gave me the date of their arrival. Rachit had only three weeks of vacation. I conveyed the message to Poonam's parents. Rachit arrived.

The first week was spent recovering from jet lag and getting his visa stamped in the passport. In the second week, we arranged for a joint meeting of both families to see if they wished to take it forward. Rachit and Poonam met for the first time.

The next morning, I asked Rachit about his opinion. He said, "I would like to meet her one-on-one." I checked with Poonam's parents. They agreed.

Rachit and Poonam met a couple more times. With just 10 days left for his return to the US and after his third meeting, when he came home, I asked about his decision. He said, "I am still thinking if she is the one with whom I can spend the rest of my life. Can I meet her once again?" I asked, "Rachit, what new things are you going to find out about her? Or what more do you want to know? This will be your last meeting with Poonam. You must tell us your decision. If it is negative, we will see other girls."

The next day, he again met Poonam, came home with just nine days left for him to go back. We were anxious to know his decision. He was cool. He said, "Give me a day to think about it." I agreed but said, "By tomorrow midnight you should give us a decision." Even Poonam's parents were anxious. It appeared that Poonam was positive about Rachit.

Now, there were exactly eight days left before he left. It was a Sunday and we had just returned from dinner. I reminded him of the midnight time limit. He told me, "I will let you know before the date changes." I read his face and it appeared to be positive. But I could only be hopeful and not certain. God forbid, were he to say no, we would have nothing to smile about.

The clock was ticking. 9 p.m., 10 p.m. Finally, at 10:15 pm, he said, "I need to talk to Rachana and Ojas." "Sure," I said as we went to the other room. He called

Rachana and Ojas to talk to them for about 35 minutes. It was now 10:50 p.m.

We asked him, "So?" He said, "I am still thinking." At 11:15 p.m., he said, "I want to talk to Rachana and Ojas once again." He talked with them. It was now 11:30 p.m. Before I could remind him that only 30 minutes were left for his final decision, he said, "I am ready." We made him repeat. He said, "Yes, I am ready and willing." I stopped him. Jaya and I hugged him, we remained just short of dancing with joy.

To date, it has remained a mystery to us. What had he to talk to Rachana and Ojas twice in about one hour? Our best speculation was and is that he respected them a lot and valued their opinion very highly.

The next morning, we called Poonam's parents to convey a 'yes' decision. They asked for some time. Within the next 10 minutes, they called us back in the affirmative. We met on the same day to decide on a simple engagement ceremony with a few close relatives and friends.

With three days remaining for Rachit to go back, the engagement ceremony was accomplished. Poonam entered our house as a daughter-in-law. A very sweet child.

At that time, she said something to me that I have kept safe in my treasure of memories.

"Pappa, thank you for accepting me into your family." Her voice was full of emotion. Her words came from the bottom of her heart. I smiled, "Welcome *beta*." But thinking, later on, I wish I could have responded as, "We are proud to have you in our family." That is a small regret.

Rachit and Poonam's wedding was solemnized a few months later. Rachana, Ojas and Parth flew in, especially for the wedding. It was another memorable event for us after Rachana and Ojas's wedding.

Rachit left after 15 days. Poonam joined him three months later. Our main responsibilities of seeing our children settled was an extraordinary feeling and an experience in itself.

CHAPTER SIXTY-EIGHT

After we discontinued brokerage activities at the Pune Stock Exchange, once in a while, I still had to visit Pune to complete the formalities of surrendering exchange membership and SEBI registration. Until we did that, the compliance requirements of regulating authorities went on increasing.

It was March 9, 2007, almost 10 years after my accident on March 1, 1997, I was visiting Pune. We rented a car with a driver known to Udaybhai. We first went to Udaybhai's vacant flat, which he had purchased a few years ago anticipating redevelopment of their Bombay building. He had already started packing his household stuff which we would carry as and when we went to Pune.

Our Dubai friend, Nitaben Dayal, who was also staying in Pune, was with us. We dropped the packed stuff at Udaybhai's house and had lunch. I had to go to the stock exchange to complete some work. I told Jaya, "I am going to the stock exchange for some work. I do not know how much time it will take. You and Nitaben proceed to her house. I will join you later on. I will take an auto-rickshaw." Jaya insisted, "We will wait in the car. Why don't you finish your work and come back?" I told her, "There is a 'No Parking' sign there. You might not be allowed to wait. You should go ahead and take a quick nap." I got down from the car and forced them to move. Jaya was reluctant but I had already turned my back to go to the exchange.

I went to the stock exchange. In about 30 minutes my work was finished. For a moment I wished I had listened to Jaya. I hired an auto-rickshaw. I had almost reached my destination, and within a minute or less, I would have reached Nitaben's house.

While the auto-rickshaw was taking a turn, I saw from the corner of my eye, a car racing towards us. Before I could tell the driver to speed up, the car ran into us at high speed. We went up into the air with tremendous impact. I was flung out of the rickshaw and hit my face on the road. Thankfully, I was not unconscious. I found my cell phone firmly held in my hand and my documents which were in a cotton bag were littered all over.

I was in tremendous pain and heard the sound of my left ankle bones being crushed. Fortunately, the last number that I dialled from my cell phone was Nitaben's which I redialled. I told them my rickshaw had met with an accident with a car on the corner of their street, asking them to come soon.

People gathered around me. They collected my documents which were strewn around. I shall remain grateful to all the Puneites forever for the help they provided. One of them even offered to take me to the hospital in his vehicle. Within a couple of minutes, Jaya and Nitaben arrived. Nitaben's son's mother-in-law, Dr Kapilaben Bharucha was to join us for tea. Her husband Dr Bharucha was in Delhi at the time. He was Medical Director in a large hospital in Pune, Jehangir Hospital. Nitaben briefed Kapilaben. She asked us to proceed to Jehangir hospital. Upon reaching the hospital, we found that she had organized everything from blood tests to x-rays.

Before we started from the accident spot, I saw a crowd gathered there, angry with the car driver and starting to beat him up. The rickshaw driver was bleeding from a wound on his head and the car driver was pretending to be in great pain to avoid a beating from the mob. I asked both of them to get into the car for urgent treatment, even though I was in unbearable pain myself. My main intention was to save the car driver from the angry crowd. I think after we reached the hospital, the auto driver might have been treated and discharged.

My x-ray revealed multiple fractures. The doctor attending on me was not an orthopaedic physician or surgeon. But he was qualified to give emergency treatment. He gave me a strong painkiller injection and plastered my left leg. I asked him, "Can I travel to Bombay?" He said, "Well, yes, if you wish. But as soon as you reach Bombay, you need to get operated upon." Kapilaben had just reached and overheard our conversation. She immediately showed the x-ray to me, insisting it was not advisable to travel to Bombay.

Meanwhile, Nitaben had talked to her husband Umeshbhai who was in Dubai. He called Dr Bharucha so he could be briefed. This was the first time I was ever admitted into a hospital and my first experience with surgery. I felt uncomfortable, if not exactly scared. I quickly resolved to put up a brave face. Did I have an option? No, was the emphatic answer.

Kapilaben told Jaya it was hard to talk to the orthopaedic surgeon who was in the operating room at that time. In the meanwhile, Rachit, Poonam, Rachana, Ojas, Udaybhai, Hansaben, and Umeshbhai, called. They all were anxious and worried. Udaybhai asked his niece, also named Nitaben (who lived in Pune) and her husband Vijaybhai, to go to the hospital. When they heard me talking normally to them thanks to painkillers, they appeared to be less worried.

I was wondering how I mustered the strength to exhibit this willpower. Was it because of the natural concern of near and dear ones? Probably yes.

Soon, Kapilaben and Jaya returned with the orthopaedic surgeon Dr Sachin Tapasvi. The attending doctor told Dr Tapasvi that I was keen to go to Bombay. He listened quietly, went through the x-ray and pathological reports.

It was 6 p.m. After a few minutes, he asked me, "What time did you have your lunch?"

"3 p.m." I said.

"Any water thereafter?"

"Few sips."

"Okay, I am operating you at 9 p.m. Any questions?"

I looked at Jaya and Kapilaben. Their faces told me I had to agree.

I told the doctor, "I have no questions."

Dr Tapasvi examined me and said, "I like your quick response. In most cases, patients waste crucial hours in making a decision. In your case, I am telling you, had you opted to travel to Bombay, your left leg would have swollen so much, no surgery would have been possible for at least a week. Medically, you would have been administered painkillers and we would need to put you under sedation for that period."

I told him, "Sir, you expressed your opinion firmly through your question. I thought it was my duty to respect your opinion. So I reciprocated quickly."

Kapilaben arranged a room meant for VVIPs for me. She left instructions with the hospital staff to take good care of me. Since I was Bombay based, I did not have enough relatives in Pune to fall back on. Meanwhile, my doctor sister-in-law Surekha, my elder sister Sarla, my nephew Prakash, brother-in-law Abu, and co-brother,

Jayant (who I have always treated as my younger brother), rushed to Pune from Bombay. They reached the hospital after I was taken to the Operation Theatre.

Before I was taken inside the Operation Theatre, a police inspector visited asking for accident details. I explained to him what exactly had happened. I did not tell him that I saw a car racing towards us. He asked me whose fault it was – the rickshaw driver or car driver?

"I don't know, Sir," I responded.

"You were in the rickshaw, is it not?"

"Sir, I was a passenger. I heard a banging sound and found myself on the road in pain."

"Okay, so give me your statement about your accident. You dictate, I will write and you have to sign the statement. This will be treated as your complaint, and it will be our job to find out whose fault it was. We have already received the rickshaw and car numbers from one of the onlookers." He then asked everyone to leave the room.

"No Sir, I do not want to file any complaint."

He looked surprised. "You have just been saved from the accident. Your leg has multiple fractures. Who knows, you may become crippled after the surgery. You are going to spend a lot of money."

"Sir, my life is saved. What more do I want?" I reasoned.

He tried to persuade me. I was firm. Sensing that I was not keen to complain, he said, "In that case, you will have to give in writing that you do not wish to complain."

"I will do that," I said.

The inspector wrote a statement on my behalf in Marathi. I could read and understand what was written. Just then, Vijaybhai, Udaybhai's sister's son-in-law came in. I requested him to read it before I signed. He read and was also surprised. He also tried to persuade me to complain. I remained firm, "No, I do not want to."

I signed the statement and had a deep sense of satisfaction. Jaya then came in and asked what had happened. I explained everything in detail to her. She agreed with me.

My main reason for not filing a complaint was purely on humanitarian grounds. I did not want the poor car and auto-rickshaw drivers to be grilled.

At the back of my mind was an incident that crossed my mind before I replied to the police inspector. A good friend of my father, a Parsi gentleman named Mr Engineer, lost his young unmarried son in a two-wheeler accident in Bombay. His son was knocked down by a BEST bus while he was waiting at the signal for it to turn green. He did not want to file a case, but many of his relatives persuaded him to ask for compensation justifying that from that amount he could do charity in his son's name. He agreed reluctantly. Just when the judge was about to deliver his verdict, Mr Engineer stood up to tell the judge, "Your honour, neither do I want any compensation, nor do I want to see the bus driver punished. I want to withdraw the case." All those present in the courtroom were stunned including the judge, who asked him, "Why? Have you been threatened?" Mr Engineer said, "No, Sir, I know how much it pains parents when they lose their child. This driver is married, has a wife, a small kid and aged parents. By seeking punishment for him, I will be asking for punishment for his entire family." The courtroom was filled with continuous clapping.

When this incident crossed my mind, I decided what I had to do.

CHAPTER SIXTY-NINE

The operation went smoothly. Surekha came into the Operating Theatre as the surgery was about to start. It lasted for about four hours. As I lay on the operating table, Dr Tapasvi jokingly said, "I am a sophisticated carpenter. I am fixing your bone furniture." The next day, at least 40 to 50 people from Bombay came to see me. The passage outside my room was noisy. Just then the matron came and requested everyone to be silent. She came into the room and said, "Dr Mrs Bharucha told me that you do not have many relatives in Pune to fall back on." I told her, "Sister, they have all come from Bombay."

I felt fortunate and blessed to have so many caring people around me.

I was discharged after three days upon my continuous insistence and transported back to Bombay. I was bedridden for three months. From the fourth month onwards, physiotherapy exercises began. From the fifth month, I was able to move about.

During this challenging period, my near and dear ones gave me strength. They visited often or called me from abroad. Udaybhai and Hansaben were regular visitors. They pampered me. I remember Udaybhai giving me a soft massage on my injured leg. Almost everyone we could call 'close family' kept me company. I told Jaya, "I think in the first month of the accident, almost everyone visited us. It included almost everyone we invited for Rachana and Rachit's wedding. Their love and feeling is our real asset."

It is said that looking at the hospital ceiling can be boring. But I was not bored even for a day. Neither did Jaya complain. And yes, with Udaybhai around, I never felt lonely and learned a thing or two about better living. It would not be an exaggeration to say that those few months were a golden period of my life, where I had a chance to introspect. It helped me in the years to come.

I want to make a quick note of something I had told Jaya. In the absence of my parents, with my brother and *bhabhi* being abroad, it was primarily our responsibility to see that our family traditions were kept alive. Jaya never made me feel, even for a second, that our family traditions were not performed. She remembered every single date on which, in the memory of our late elders, priests were to be invited, given gifts, just as my mother did. My contribution towards maintaining these traditions was a big zero.

Time went by quickly. Thanks to Stephen Covey and his book, I began thinking beyond who did what to me, who said what about us. I do not know how, but he became a meticulous magician performing a fancy trick in transforming my life. In my mind, I set up my thought process in the right direction. Even today, I wonder how easily I became exceptionally good at battling a powerful and deadly enemy – EGO – emerging victorious. This proved to be a key in my being joyous and cheerful, self-satisfied and content ever since.

I was not disturbed. I did not feel hurt. I stopped expecting anything from anyone. I also trained myself to be detached from things and people if I felt it disturbed me. It was hard to practice. After all, I am also human. But by remaining determined, I ultimately was able to master the art. Remaining detached does not mean you break all relationships, you keep a distance without making it obvious.

Everyone has some problem or the other. If anyone came to me to ask for help, I would eagerly help them with my God-given prudence. Those problems could be financial, family-related, legal, or social. Because of my mediation, I was able to solve many problems.

I am willing to accept the guilt of self-praise. I have never said no to anyone seeking my help, even if they have hurt me in the past. With all sincerity and honesty, I have tried to help them out. By doing this, I had a sense of satisfaction within me.

My formula to resolve conflicts was simple – invite all parties to help them communicate directly and make them understand the accuracy of stories rather than believing the stories told to them by someone else. One needs to understand the reasons why circumstances changed suddenly or why things happened. Then finding a solution is easy.

I have become immune to both good and bad opinions, but not at the cost of self-respect and family. These two are my top priorities. But that does not mean I don't feel hurt or argue with people who challenge me. What I am doing is to add such people to my detachment list, without being obvious. By doing that, I make sure I do not feel hurt or disturbed. Try this, life will be beautiful.

CHAPTER SEVENTY

Rachana and Ojas were blessed with a sweet daughter, Parami. For some time now, I was thinking about retirement. Now that the children were settled, could I opt for retiring from the business? Jaya and I started discussing this possibility. But what would we do after that? We shared our thoughts with Udaybhai and Hansaben. They endorsed our thinking. It was time, but we were uncertain when exactly it would happen.

One day Rachit and Poonam called us. "Pappa, how about taking it easy now? You have done enough. Live a relaxed life now. If you do business for long, then when will we get yours and mummy's time?"

I replied, "I have also been thinking of that for some time now. Let me mull over it."

They went on, "Pappa, we are there. Do not worry about anything. You can spend maximum time with us in the USA."

I said, "Let me think."

Coincidentally or planned by children, after a few days, even Rachana and Ojas touched upon the same subject. Both of them said, "Pappa, we, Rachit and Poonam can now take care of everything. Do not worry about anything."

I said, "Let me think."

During our next visit to the USA, we discussed it jointly. All the children – Ojas, Rachana, Rachit and Poonam – expected me to agree to spend more time with them. Jaya and I decided that it was our turn to respect their feelings. I told them, "Okay, I have decided to call it a day. Give me some time to formally announce my retirement. It will not take me more than a year."

Soon, Rachit and Poonam were blessed with a son, Param.

A ton of load was off my mind. I thank God for such lovely and loving children. I could not have wished for more at the age of 60.

I happened to speak to Jethabhai with whom I had an excellent relationship, even outside of the market. At first, he didn't believe me, thinking I was joking. When I told him I mean it, he said, "Had there been any other person in your place, I would not have taken him seriously. I sincerely wish you do not take such a decision. When do you plan to retire?"

I replied, "I have not decided on a date, but it could be soon… in about six months."

Somehow word spread in the market. Everyone with whom I was friendly asked me about my decision, wondering what had happened. Some of them even jumped to conclusions. They would say, "I support you in all respects." I smiled saying, "Nothing has happened. My children insist that we spend more time with them." I never gave any further explanation. On specific queries about problems with partners, "Nothing of that sort" was my standard reply.

Rachana, Ojas and the children were to visit India during Diwali which was six months away.

I decided to formally announce my decision to my partners soon. Meanwhile, I saw a huge swing in my moods – from gloom to jubilation. I would say that both are uniquely different.

I invited my partners home to inform them of my decision to quit the partnership and business. I knew that they were aware of this, just did not know the date. I told them, "It is the children's wish which I have decided to honour and respect to spend more time with them." They looked at each other and suggested continuing for at least three months. "Think again. You continue but you can stay away from the business for those three months before a final decision is made." I saw no point in delaying but agreed with their request. I also told them that the chance of changing my decision was remote at best. I told them that in case they needed my physical presence at the shop on account of any emergency, I would help out.

Three months before the year-end, I stopped going to the shop. After another two months, I went to the market to tell fellow suppliers, traders, brokers about my quitting from a particular date. Almost all of them tried to convince me not to retire giving me unsolicited advice, citing examples of people who took a similar decision and were unhappy.

They thought I might have had problems with the partnership. To counter that, I continued going to the market for at least a few hours. Everyone was convinced that there was nothing wrong except a senior supplier, Narottambhai, who had seen my partner's family parting ways with their partners.

He asked me, "What went wrong?"

I said, "Nothing, I have not had any problem."

He kept going, "I know you are not the one who would create problems but…"

I interrupted him. "Sir, let us stop here."

Another young supplier of studded silver jewellery, Nandubhai, had tremendous respect for me. Only he could answer why. When I informed him, he said, "I know you are joking. I tried to impress on him that I was serious and if he wanted to verify from so-and-so …"

He only said, "Whenever I meet you, you always make me happy. Today for the first time you made me cry." He walked out. Some of them even started spending more time with me either at the market or requesting me to go out with them for breakfast, tea and lunch.

Everybody's love and affection took me back to the days when I had decided to quit my job in Dubai. The only difference was that I was in a great dilemma then even when it was a conscious decision. I was uncertain about the future with responsibilities on my shoulders such as ageing parents, children's education, their careers, seeing them married off and raising a family. Now, I had no such responsibilities. Both my children were happy and settled in their married life. They were also firmly established in their career. They would be the rocks solidly behind us in any eventuality. How many parents were as fortunate as us? Our son-in-law and daughter-in-law were a son and daughter to us. And we are Pappa and Mummy to them. What more do we expect from God? He has been more than kind to us.

Looking around, we see the plight of many parents who in their later life were saddened by the attitude of their children.

Many times I think to myself – "Is life by itself easy, difficult or painful?" It has the basic characteristic of having conflicting answers. It depends on at what stage or age you attempt to answer.

Many such parents complained about their children. It was indeed painful to even hear that. Sadly, other than extending them a sympathetic ear, there is nothing more I could do. I was taking special care to help them in whatever way I could – advising them on personal and medical issues, helping them to make their will and so on. They would also tell us how lucky we were to have such wonderful children. Hearing this, Jaya and I always felt proud of our children. In most cases, I knew the root cause – expectations. If you rise above your expectations, you will be happy.

CHAPTER SEVENTY-ONE

Rachana, Parth and Parami visited for a short vacation that coincided with Diwali. She wanted to be with us at Diwali as it had not been possible for many years. Now that I was free, I enjoyed my time with them by being with them all the time. I informed Rachana that I had decided to retire from active business. She was delighted. She immediately told Ojas, Rachit and Poonam. They congratulated me for finally taking a crucial, but long overdue decision. I told them, "It was all your love, care and support that enabled me to take such a decision. I give you all the credit to make our life easier from here on out." In no uncertain terms, they expressed their happiness that now we would be able to spend more time with them in the USA.

Almost three months had passed. I had announced my retirement not knowing what I was going to do while in India. But I knew my engagement in social activities along with my hobby of reading and writing would keep me sufficiently occupied. Meanwhile, many suppliers enquired if I was planning to start my own business. If so, they stated that they would like to deal with me. I told them that I had no immediate plans, but if I decided to do so in the future, I would let them know.

I received many calls from people in the market asking me to join them, all of which I politely declined. One day, I got a call from a client Sudhaben Shah. She said, "Vijaybhai, whenever I visit your shop you are not to be seen."

I said, "I have retired from the shop. I come to the market twice or thrice a week, but only during early evening hours."

She seemed surprised.

She went on, "Are you starting your own business?"

I told her, I wasn't planning on doing so.

Immediately she said, "If you are not starting your own, I will go to other shops."

I asked her, "Why? What went wrong?"

She answered, "I was coming to your shop because of you, and it is not the same without you."

Thanking her, I said, "Give me a few days to think. I will let you know."

I spoke with Jaya. She said, "It is your wish. But there is no harm if we start our own."

Later that evening, another client called me.

She asked, "Why have you not been seen at the shop?"

I shared with her that I had retired.

She also sounded a bit surprised.

After a brief pause, she continued, "Vijaybhai, do you remember many years back, I walked into your shop with my father. The way you attended on us and guided us to start a gemstone business, my father had told me thereafter that 'as long as Vijaybhai is there to do the business, you will be safe and not be misguided'. After my father died, with your support I was able to carry on our gems business. Many times I was getting offers from the other shopkeepers in your market, but I never even stepped into any other shop. Ever. Now, what should I do?"

My answer was simple. "Continue to go to the shop. They know you. You know the rates. Where is the problem?"

She said, "Dealing with you is so easy. I never realized I am dealing with a trader. Sometimes in your absence, your other partners helped me, but I want to work with you."

In our line of business, it is like that. Once you are comfortable with someone in the shop, you always want to deal with the same person.

"So, what should I do?" she continued. "If you decide not to restart your business, I will shut my business as advised by my late father." She sounded nervous. "Vijaybhai, you know my family's financial situation."

All I could say after that was, "Let me think it over. I will get back to you in a few days."

I briefed Jaya again. She again said, "There is no harm if we start our own."

We discussed logistics, investments, how to service clients etc. We concluded that the initial investment would not be much as all the suppliers would give us goods on approval. Regarding how to service the clients, we could think of only two options – either I visit their home or office or they came to our house. We also decided that I should not spend the whole day on the job. Maybe four or five hours a day maximum including travel time.

I called Sudhaben. Jocularly I told her, "If I start my own business, would you be able to come to my house which is about 25+ km from yours?"

"I will do that," was her instant reply.

I then said, "I was just joking. When can we meet?"

She said, "Tomorrow around 3 p.m. at my residence?"

I agreed.

Before going to her house, I first went to the market to talk to some of the suppliers. I informed them that I was planning to start my own business. I asked them if they would be willing to give goods to me on an approval basis. I reminded them that I would not have a brand name for my firm.

Without exception, they said, "Please do not insult us by telling that. We have a great amount of faith in you. We respect you." One of them went a step ahead and said, "Doing business with you will be a great pleasure and honour for me."

I was sitting in my supplier's office when I said to him, "Look, I do not have a shop or office in the market. All of you have seen my house when you visited me after my accident. I do not even have a nameplate. What if sometimes I need an expensive item for approval?"

He responded, "Vijaybhai, our stock is yours. I am assuring you of mine as well as on behalf of the others present here." Everyone nodded in agreement. "You will have no problem with suppliers irrespective of the value of goods." All present echoed the words.

I was humbled, and told them, "Thank you very much. I may visit you anytime from tomorrow."

They expressed happiness.

With reassurance from the suppliers, I went straight to Sudhaben's house to keep my 3 p.m. appointment. She and her husband were waiting for me. Her husband was a man of few words. He kept quiet while she and I discussed a certain design which she had kept ready. After exchanging and understanding each other's views and making some amendments, she finally approved the design of that particular item.

I told her, "Sudhaben, I will be going to America in a few days and will return in about three months. Are you in a hurry?" She said no and asked me when I would return. When I told her, she said, "Okay. Call me as soon as you are back in India."

On the morning of my return to India, she called me to confirm my meeting with her.

We were sipping coffee as we talked. She wanted an estimate which I gave her. She instantly approved it. "Go ahead and make it." I thanked her and gave her a tentative date by which it should be ready.

Just as I was about to leave, she said, "Just a minute." And glanced at her husband. He went inside a room and returned with a package. She said, "Take this as an advance payment." I told her, "Thank you very much, but you know even in the shop I would never accept any advance. I want to continue that practice. However, if I need it, I will let you know."

She looked at her husband and remarked, "This is the Vijaybhai I know."

I thanked her again for the gesture. I must admit that I did not know this side of Sudhaben. She offered an advance realizing I was now doing business independently. I appreciated her understanding. Today I have no hesitation in saying that it was Mrs Sudhaben Shah who was instrumental in pushing me to start my own business. Now our relationship is beyond business. We have become family friends.

I went home and briefed Jaya about my meeting with Sudhaben. We were happy to have received the first order of my independent business.

My retirement from the partnership led to the success of my independent business. It was proven by satisfactory growth, even when I was selective about the clients I wanted to work with. I experienced that it was always difficult to live a smooth life with honesty. To do so, one needs a comprehensive dedication to the truth. If one got used to living a life with these two basics – honesty and truth, rewards would be sweet and unimaginable.

During my business journey, I found that some people were natural liars and hypocrites. They did more harm to themselves than to others. Their lies in business caused irreparable damage to their social status.

I took the approach to not allow my valuable social assets to be depreciated or converted into liabilities. I was able to figure out the practical consequences specific to me. Fortunately, after retiring from my partnership, I understood my past perfectly. Therefore anticipating the future was an easy task. I did not allow myself to meet challenges with contradictory thoughts. I had a firm determination to beat the odds and challenges encountered. That enabled me not to live a mysterious and confusing life.

CHAPTER SEVENTY-TWO

Before I end my journey, however, I cannot resist the temptation to share a couple of memorable incidents that reflected love, respect, faith and trust in me by some clients.

During one of my visits to the USA, a week after I got there, an elderly client, Ekta Khadse, called me. Some of my more regular clients had my USA contact number.

"When did you leave for the USA?" she asked me.

"About a week ago," I responded.

"How long will you be there for?"

"Approximately four months."

"Oh, God! I have some work for you."

"Tell me. What is it?"

"I want to present rings with a solitaire to my son and daughter-in-law who will be celebrating their silver wedding anniversary."

Sensing her urgency, I said, "Okay, I will guide you where to go…"

"No, no, when are you returning?" she asked again.

"Approximately after four months. When is their anniversary?"

"Next month."

"Okay, I will give you some numbers. Call them. Your work will be done. You will get good stuff."

"No, I want you to select the diamonds. You make the rings and deliver to me personally," she insisted.

I pushed back, "I think that it will be difficult. If you want me to give it to you personally, then it will not be possible. I am so sorry."

"Vijaybhai, you have disappointed me. Let me think. I will call you back in half an hour."

After 15 minutes she called. She sounded cheerful.

"*Aare bhai* listen. I spoke to my son who is in Kuwait. I told him what I wished to present them on their silver wedding anniversary. I also told him that Vijaybhai is not here. He is in the USA and he will come back only after four months. And you know I do not buy anything from anyone else ever since I met him. So on your silver wedding anniversary, I will give you blessings and you will have to consider that I have already given you the gifts. When *bhai* returns, he will make the rings and then I will give them to you. Is that okay? And you know *bhai*, what my son said? 'It is okay Mom, we need just your blessings'. I was relaxed. So when you come back, do my job first."

"Definitely. It will be my responsibility to complete the job as early as possible when I return," I assured her. She was very happy.

For the next three hours, I did not say a word. I pretended to be relaxing. What trust, what confidence was shown to me!

I wished, God willing, I stay blessed always.

When I returned to India, I made the rings and handed them over to her. I cannot forget the expression on her face–full of love for me, who she considered a younger brother.

When her son visited, they organized a family get-together. I was invited. Her son asked me, "Vijaybhai, what magic have you done on my mother?"

I said, "It is her magnanimity to have such trust in me. You also deserve appreciation for recognizing her feelings and wish."

He said, "Vijaybhai, I am just kidding." He hugged me. I felt lots of warmth in it.

Thereafter, whenever she had any work, however small, even a minor repair job, I would collect the items from her, fix them and return them to her at her house. I would not calculate my travel and miscellaneous expenses in exchange for taking her blessings.

My network of clients started developing – a few were old customers from when I was at the shop. The rest were new.

I soon found that sometimes I was doing better than at the shop. I believed in doing business with pleasure and remaining one hundred per cent ethical. I never compromised on that. I adhered to my resolution of not working for more than four to five hours a day including travel time for the business. This gave me a lot of flexible hours to devote to my other hobbies like reading and writing. I was able to do business with clients who would not treat me like an ordinary trader, and who never pressured me for anything.

I could also afford to remain selective about adding new clients to my network. If any new client sounded like they were treating me just like another trader, I politely declined to accept their business. If any existing clients showed signs of such developments, I managed to create and maintain a business distance from them under one pretext or another.

That reminds me...

A very good client of mine, Parag Thakur and his wife, a middle-aged couple approached me to make a diamond necklace set for their daughter's wedding, which was to take place four months later. Their daughter was in the UK. They visited my house, selected a design, approved the estimate and pulled out a chequebook to pay me an advance. I politely said, "I do not want any advance." They said, "By giving you this cheque we feel that we have started our wedding shopping. It is considered auspicious." I thought for a while and said, "Okay, in that case, I accept the cheque." As they were getting up, he said, "Vijaybhai, we trust you fully as we do not know anything about diamonds." I looked at them and told them to please sit down for a few more minutes. They reoccupied their chairs.

I said, "Paragbhai, I cannot undertake this particular order."

He was shocked. "Why? What happened? Have I said something wrong?"

I said, "No, you have not, but maybe I have misunderstood. I accept I am wrong."

Both husband and wife looked at each other in disbelief.

He again asked, "What is it? We don't understand."

I replied, "For all these years, whatever you made with me, you have never said 'we trust you'. But today when you said those words, I felt that in your subconscious you thought 'what if I tell you something and deliver something else?' As a customer, you are right to express your concern. I should only be saying, don't worry. I will take care. But somehow I feel otherwise and have decided not to execute your order."

He said, "I did not mean that."

I said, "When I sense even a 1% deficiency in trust, consciously or unconsciously, I cannot work in that atmosphere."

He said, "No, Vijaybhai. We assure you we fully trust you."

I remained firm. "Paragbhai, we have had an excellent relationship so far and I wish to continue that. So, I will not make this particular item. But, in making this item, I am offering you my help whenever you need it. From the selection of diamonds to the finished product. Or, if you want to buy it ready-made, I can come with you or give my opinion."

Both, Paragbhai and his wife, began to apologize. I told them, "You need not offer any apology. As a customer, it is your right to get assurance and reassurance from the trader. It is me who has to apologize for not being able to execute your order."

When they saw that I was firm, they left, disturbed, unhappy and to some extent maybe even angry with me. Why not? They were justified.

After a month, I received a call from Paragbhai, "Can I meet you?"

"Welcome," is all I said.

"Is around 7 p.m. today convenient for you?"

"Sure, I will be waiting for you."

I thought to myself that maybe they had shortlisted some items and wanted my opinion.

At exactly 7 p.m., they came home. After exchanging pleasantries, we were having snacks and tea. Neither they nor I opened the topic which I had closed when we last met. They were my guests. I could not ask them the reason for coming over. We were talking generally – global, domestic affairs, politics and economics.

When we were done, I thought I now needed to break the ice and so I asked, "How are preparations for the wedding going?"

He said, "I want to show you something." He pulled out a printout from his pocket requesting me to take a look at it.

I took it and read:

Dear Papa, Mama,

Please inform Vijay uncle that if he refuses to make jewellery for me, I will not wear any jewellery on my wedding day.

I took a while to control my emotions and be calm. When I finally looked up I told Paragbhai, "I will execute the order."

Hearing my response, Paragbhai said, "That day, my wife and I tried hard to convince you, but you remained adamant and today…"

I interrupted him and said, "Between those three lines I could see the face of my daughter."

They both went away happy and satisfied.

I poured my heart into making that diamond set since she was to wear it on her wedding day. When it was ready, I was satisfied with the finished product. I went to deliver the set about three weeks before the wedding date. My co-brother, Jayantbhai, was with me.

They invited us into their house. However, before opening the box, Paragbhai and his wife, both bowed down to touch my feet. I simply smiled and gestured to say, "God Bless You."

Paragbhai said, "Vijaybhai, you have not yet cashed the cheque given to you as an advance."

I told them, "You wanted to give me an advance so that you feel that you have started wedding shopping. It was your belief. I did not want any advance. So both our considerations were preserved."

They handed over an envelope to me. Then they opened the box. "Beautiful, Vijaybhai. It looks bigger. You have made some changes, haven't you?"

I answered in the affirmative.

"And what is the new bill?"

I told them, "It is there in the box. Let the wedding get over. Your daughter should like it. Her husband and in-laws should also like it. In the event they do not like this design, I will remake it."

They thanked me. We came down. I remembered the envelope they gave me. I opened it. It was a blank signed cheque in my name.

Jayantbhai told me, "I have seen a second such client who bows to you in respect. We have to plead with our customers for payment. It is just the reverse with you."

I smiled. I thought maybe my way of doing business was different and not along the expected lines of common practice. This had enabled me to develop new relations on a solid cemented base of mutual trust and respect.

Before writing the amount on the cheque, I called Paragbhai to let him know the figure. He asked me, "This is less than the estimate you had originally given us and the set looks bigger too!"

I told him that I got the goods at the most reasonable rates. He did not argue on the phone and simply said, "Bless my daughter that she will have a happy married life. She and her husband and in-laws are very happy with the set."

What I did not indicate to him was that I did not add a single penny as my profit. This I had decided when I read the note she had written to her parents.

Dear Papa, Mama,

Please inform Vijay uncle that if he refuses to make jewellery for me, I will not wear any jewellery on my wedding day.

Between those three lines, I could see the face of my daughter.

□

It is not the end, life goes on.

Made in the USA
Las Vegas, NV
31 July 2021

27359811R00204